BREAKING
DOWN PLATH

BREAKING
DOWN PLATH

PATRICIA GRISAFI

JB JOSSEY-BASS™
A Wiley Brand

Jossey-Bass
A Wiley Imprint
111 River St, Hoboken, NJ 07030
www.josseybass.com

Jossey-Bass books and products are available through most bookstores. To contact Jossey-Bass directly, call our Customer Care Department within the U.S. at 800–956–7739, outside the U.S. at +1 317 572 3986, or fax +1 317 572 4002.

Wiley also publishes its books in a variety of electronic formats and by print-on-demand. Some material included with standard print versions of this book may not be included in e-books or in print-on-demand. If this book refers to media such as a CD or DVD that is not included in the version you purchased, you may download this material at http://booksupport.wiley.com. For more information about Wiley products, visit www.wiley.com.

Library of Congress Cataloging-in-Publication Data is Available:

ISBN 9781119782384 (Paperback)
ISBN 9781119782391 (ePDF)
ISBN 9781119782407 (ePub)

COVER ART & DESIGN: PAUL MCCARTHY

SKY10032200_122821

For my son Damien

Contents

Foreword

In "Context," a short work of prose published in *The London Magazine* in February 1962, Sylvia Plath discusses how the issues of her time impact on her writing. It concludes eloquently:

> Surely the great use of poetry is its pleasure—not its influence as religious or political propaganda. Certain poems and lines of poetry seem as solid and miraculous to me as church altars or the coronation of queens must seem to people who revere quite different images. I am not worried that poems reach relatively few people. As it is, they go surprisingly far—among strangers, around the world, even. Farther than the words of a classroom teacher or the prescriptions of a doctor; if they are lucky, farther than a lifetime.

Sylvia Plath endures. She holds our attention, and as a result, people all over the world think about her, recite her poetry, and write articles, essays, and books about her. Her novel *The Bell Jar* (1963) has been translated into more than thirty-five languages, including Braille. Yet, fifty-eight years after her death, we find we still have much to learn about Plath the person *and* Plath the writer.

The recent publication of the more than 1,400 letters Plath composed helps to fuel our interest in her. When combined with her poetry, prose, and other life writing, an astoundingly prolific and diverse person develops who defies singular classification. Plath's output in various genres of writing and media of expression make her an endlessly fascinating area of study.

Patricia Grisafi's *Breaking Down Plath* is up to the moment. It blends historical and contemporary readings of Sylvia Plath—the major themes in her poetry and important aspects of her prose—in such a way that you, her newest readers, will understand and relate to the mid-twentieth century's most famous writer.

Peter K. Steinberg, co-editor of *The Letters of Sylvia Plath*
11 February 2021

Acknowledgments

Many thanks to my team at Jossey-Bass for its support, guidance, and assistance during this process: Riley Harding, Christine O'Connor, and Kezia Endsley. I am grateful to Maria Farland for helping make the opportunity to write a book on Sylvia Plath a reality. An extra big thank you to Peter K. Steinberg for your help; you are an invaluable resource and incredibly generous with your time and knowledge. To Gail Crowther, Fox Frazier Foley, and Li Yun Alvarado, thank you for your helpful feedback, suggestions, and notes on early versions of this project. Cristina Baptista, thank you for your insightful commentary and advice; you truly went above and beyond. To my writing group Erin Khar, Naomi Rand, and Amy Klein: thank you for providing editorial assistance and emotional support. Thank you to The Plath Society for organizing all of the Zoom events that kept Plath scholars and fans connected during the pandemic. I am grateful for the Plath community, especially Julie Goodspeed-Chadwick, Dave Haslam, Emily Van Duyne, and Elizabeth Winder. Thank you to Jake Currie for being flexible with my work schedule so I could complete this book. To the Ladies' Group Text—Lauren Navarro, Sophia Chang, and Deborah Schwarz—you guys are a lifeline. Thank you to my therapist, Lisa Youngclaus, for your continued encouragement. Many thanks to my childcare professional, Tashi Sherpa: Without your hard work, it would have been impossible to write this book. Mom and Dad, I am grateful for your continued support and belief in me. To all the writers, teachers, artists, and scholars continuing to bring Sylvia Plath's work to wider audiences: Keep up the wonderful work. As always, thank you to my husband, Scott Goldstein, for reading many drafts of this book and being a truly supportive partner. I could not have done this without you.

About the Author

Patricia Grisafi, PhD, is a freelance writer, editor, and educator. She received her BA in English from Skidmore College and her PhD in English from Fordham University. She lives in New York City with her husband, son, and two rescue dogs.

Introduction

When I was a sophomore in high school, I couldn't wait to study Sylvia Plath. I had been reading her work on my own for years and was excited to finally get the chance to dig in with my teacher and fellow students. In the massive *Modern American Literature* textbook, though, there was only one Plath poem: "Mirror." It's a fine poem, but it's short and safe; it doesn't ruffle any feathers. Our teacher discussed its themes, talked a little bit about Plath's life, and mentioned that she "died young." That was it.

I couldn't believe it. In a classroom where we studied at least ten Robert Frost poems and seemingly everything Ralph Waldo Emerson wrote, couldn't we at least read one more Plath poem? (No disrespect to Mr. Frost and Mr. Emerson, of course.)

Today, Sylvia Plath is everywhere. Her name has its own connotation—we associate "Plathian" with anything dark, witty, and shocking. You can buy Sylvia Plath magnets for the fridge and Sylvia Plath socks for a cold night. Plath quotes make good T-shirt designs. There is an Instagram account dedicated to fans who have gotten Plath tattoos. Lady Gaga and Lana Del Rey, among other musicians, have referred to her in their songs. A 2003 movie was made about her starring Gwyneth Paltrow. Plath is also often mentioned in films focused on teenagers. For example, in *Spider-Man: Homecoming* (2017), MJ (played by Zendaya) is wearing a Plath T-shirt. It functions as a shortcut to understanding MJ's personality: She's a little morbid, no-nonsense, and into female empowerment.

While Sylvia Plath is now so well-known she's actually become commoditized, it wasn't always that way. When she died, she was not a household name—not even close. It wasn't until the posthumous publication of *Ariel* that she became iconic. Over the years, the ways we approach Sylvia Plath's work have shifted, which allows her reputation as an integral writer in American literature to grow. Despite the near-mythological status she now occupies across film, fashion, and digital media, Plath was first and foremost a woman who wrote. Plath viewed herself as a writer from a young age, and her identity intertwined with writing for her whole life. In a journal entry she wrote at age seventeen, Plath called herself "the girl who wanted to be God"—a phrase that speaks to her ambitious nature.

Plath had many identities—some contradictory. She was a dutiful daughter who also struggled to liberate herself from her family. She was a hard-working and brilliant student who enjoyed parties and fashion. She was an *expatriate*—an American who moved to England. She was a wife who wanted to get out of her husband's shadow. She was a mother who wanted to be seen as both a loving parent and a successful career woman. And she was a person who lived with mental illness and died by suicide.

Plath has always spoken to young people, people who feel disenchanted with their world, people who feel deeply and are passionate about life, who feel like they don't belong. She taps into our rage and our joy in a unique way. When I was that disappointed high school student who wanted more Plath and less Emerson, I wondered why the teachers kept her from us. Was she too intense? Too taboo? Not appropriate for high school students? Why did we read *The Catcher in the Rye* and not *The Bell Jar*?

It turns out Plath is more than appropriate—she is necessary. In our contemporary moment, which shares many uncomfortable commonalities with Plath's World War II and Cold War upbringing, Plath's voice is more urgent than ever. For those struggling with mental health issues, she reminds us that we can choose how to define ourselves and our disabilities. For those angry about the prevalence of rape culture, she reminds us that our voices matter and that they can give us power. For those who feel like they don't belong, she reminds us that we can find our people. She reminds us that the personal is still political, that the political is also personal.

Chapter 1
Who Was Sylvia Plath?

PLATH'S CHILDHOOD

Plath was born in Boston, Massachusetts, on October 27, 1932, to Aurelia Schober Plath and Otto Plath. Aurelia was a second-generation American of Austrian descent, and Otto was an immigrant from Germany. Otto's German heritage would play a huge role in Plath's self-conception as a middle-class New Englander.

Aurelia was a teacher, and Otto was a professor who specialized in bees. He even wrote an influential book, *Bumblebees and Their Ways* (1934). Sylvia had a brother, Warren, who was two years younger. This would be their family unit until Otto Plath's untimely—and ultimately preventable—death when Sylvia was eight.

Otto Plath suffered from diabetes but ignored his condition until his leg had to be medically amputated. Afterward, his health plummeted, his amputation became infected, and he died of complications due to diabetes. Otto's death would haunt Sylvia for the rest of her life.

Sylvia would later write about how idyllic her childhood had been until her father's death in the essay "Ocean 1212-W": "And this is how it stiffens, my vision of that seaside childhood. My father died, we moved inland. Whereon those nine first years of my life sealed themselves off like a ship in a bottle—beautiful, inaccessible, obsolete, a fine, white flying myth." Ultimately, her father's death would shape Sylvia's relationships with men, religion, politics, and herself, and would be the basis for some of her most powerful poetry.

After Otto's death, Aurelia moved the family away from its home in the seaside town of Winthrop, Massachusetts, inland to the suburbs of Wellesley. There, Sylvia lived in a multigenerational home with her maternal grandparents. Aurelia always managed to make ends meet, but the family had to be frugal. Aware that she wasn't as financially privileged as other children in the neighborhood, Sylvia—already showing signs of precocious intelligence—became an overachiever and a perfectionist. She spent most of her middle and high school years winning academic awards and accumulating scholarships.

A SCHOLARSHIP GIRL

Plath started at prestigious Smith College in 1950 on a scholarship sponsored by writer Olive Higgins Prouty. Plath was keenly aware of class stratifications at the elite, all-women's college. She put intense pressure on herself to be perfect. Writing in her journal on October 1, 1957, Plath addresses a "demon" who is in reality her "murderous self" who demands perfection: "Not being perfect hurts," she writes. "This is the month which ends a quarter of a century for me, lived under the shadow of fear: fear that I would fall short of some abstract perfection: I have often fought, fought & won, not perfection, but an acceptance of myself as having a right to live on my own human, fallible terms" (*Unabridged Journals*, 2000, p. 618).

This need to be perfect is a personality characteristic, but it's also a value very much encouraged during Plath's life. Throughout the 1950s, as we will learn further in the next chapter, in Plath's social circles there was a lot of stress on appearances and conformity—especially for women. Sylvia, always a savvy observer of double standards, participated in many of the rituals of college life at this time while criticizing them in her writing. She went to formal dances, had many dates and friends, and immersed herself in studies and activities. Well-liked, incredibly bright, and fiercely ambitious, Sylvia Plath looked like she had everything going for her.

But mental illness is insidious. For someone with a predisposition to depression, as Plath had, it can feel like everything is wrong and will never get better. Mental healthcare was much less sophisticated in the 1950s than it is today, and conversations about mental health in general were often conducted in hushed tones, as if struggling with one's emotions was something about which to be ashamed. The stigma of mental illness prevented many people from getting the proper treatment. Women especially, who often were dismissed by male doctors, felt disempowered when it came to medical care, especially gynecological and psychiatric care.

Plath grappled with suicidal ideation and feelings of depression and worthlessness for most of her adult life. Her mental health struggles formed some of her most powerful poems. An understanding of Plath's mental health—and how she conceived of it—is valuable to any study of her work, but we need to be careful not to pathologize her or her poetry.

THE RISKS OF READING AUTOBIOGRAPHICALLY

It is tempting to read Plath's work as purely autobiographical, as several scholars have done in the past. However, as Plath studies evolve, we now understand that reading Plath's work from a solely autobiographical perspective poses problems and closes off the work from its larger contexts. We must always think of Plath as a writer who used autobiographical elements in her work and transformed them into art. In short, her real-life experiences informed her art—but are not necessarily the only aspects of the writing itself.

While Plath mined her life for inspiration, her work stands on its own. Plath never intended to write an autobiography; she carefully chose poetry and fiction as her medium with a few short essays written toward the end of her life. "Rather than assume that Plath is an unusually autobiographical writer," Plath critic Susan R. Van Dyne notes, "we need to understand that she experienced her life in unusually textual ways. In her letters and journals as much as in her fiction and poetry, Plath's habits of self-representation suggest that she regarded her life as if it were a text she could invent and rewrite" (Van Duyne, 1993, p. 5). Plath kept journals. She composed letters. She wrote fiction. She crafted poetry. She was familiar with all mediums and made artistic choices fitting to each one. To only read Plath as an autobiographical writer would be to miss out on the myriad layers in her work. Therefore, readers should bear in mind the distinction between the speaker/narrator and the author when reading, and refrain from pathological narratives and unfounded mental health diagnoses.

A TURNING POINT

In 1953, Plath's life took a series of twists that would ultimately lead to a suicide attempt. Aside from academic success (Plath was elected to Phi Beta Kappa and also learned she would be the editor of the *Smith Review* for her senior year), Plath won a guest editorship position at *Mademoiselle* magazine, which she held during the summer at its New York City offices. She and other winners were put up at a women's-only hotel, The Barbizon, and were expected to fulfill their duties as well as put forward a positive face representing the magazine while touring the city.

Plath drew inspiration from this experience in her only published novel, *The Bell Jar* (1963). Aside from the novel, some letters, and scant journal entries, we don't know a lot about this time during Plath's life from Plath's own perspective. However, once she finished her editorship, returned home, and received a rejection from a Harvard University writing program she desperately wanted to take, her mental health seemed to take a dive.

Facing a long stretch of summer vacation at home with her mother and nothing to look forward to, Plath fell into a deep depression that was so severe it had physical effects. Unable to sleep, read, or write, Plath reached out for help. Her mother took her to a male psychiatrist, and that psychiatrist gave her improperly administered electroconvulsive therapy (ECT). In *The Bell Jar*, Plath would compare the experience to how one must feel being electrocuted and tortured. This event would haunt Plath and her writing for the rest of her life, coming up again and again as an image and metaphor in her poetry.

Plath's condition continued to deteriorate. On August 24, 1953, Plath consumed a bottle of pills and hid in a crawlspace in the basement. She was unconscious for two days, during which an exhaustive search took place throughout the greater Boston area. Her disappearance made the newspapers: "Beautiful Smith Girl Missing at Wellesley," read the headline of *The Boston Daily Globe*. "Mrs. Aurelia S. Plath, of 26 Elmwood Street, said her daughter apparently left the house at 2 p.m., leaving a note saying she was 'taking a long walk' and would 'be back tomorrow.'"

Plath was found in the crawlspace with injuries to her face from hitting her head. She was treated and hospitalized at McLean Hospital, a private hospital in Boston renowned for its psychiatry program. Plath's Smith College benefactor Olive Higgins Prouty helped pay for most of Plath's care. Prouty herself had suffered a nervous breakdown and could relate to Plath's struggles. As part of her

Figure 1.1 Plath at the beach, 1954.
Source: Bridgeman Images

treatment, Plath received regular therapy sessions, which she found beneficial, with Dr. Ruth Barnhouse Beuscher. She received ECT again, but this time it was administered correctly and actually helped Plath's depression. Plath's work with Dr. Beuscher gave her the tools she needed to manage her mental health and eventually return to school. The two of them would remain in contact for the rest of Plath's life.

After her recovery, Plath threw herself back into college life with fervor—and started to hone her skills and develop the poetic voice that would earn her a respected place in American literature. She finished her college education with high honors and received a Fulbright Scholarship, which would allow her to study English at Newnham College, Cambridge University. She would seek further education abroad, which was not the norm for women during this time.

As an American in England during the 1950s, Plath experienced culture shock—her brash Americanness sometimes uncomfortably set her apart. Acquaintance Jane Baltzell remembered Plath seemed "totally unaware of how her American behavior and talk seemed rather comic to the British" (Wilson, 2013, p. 292). However, she was also exposed to new poets who greatly influenced her—including her future husband Ted Hughes. She had to adjust to a new way of life, a new educational system, and a new set of expected behaviors.

MEETING TED HUGHES

When Sylvia met Ted Hughes in 1956, he had published a few poems in university publications and already was garnering a reputation for powerful and violent poetry about the natural world and human relationships. When the two first met in 1956 at a wild party famously recounted in Plath's journals, she recited bits of his poetry to him. Then, they passionately kissed and Hughes snatched Plath's headband and earrings: "I was stamping and he was stamping on the floor, and then he kissed me bang smash on the mouth and ripped my hairband off. . .and when he kissed my neck I bit him long and hard on the cheek" (*Unabridged Journals*, 2000, p. 212).

Plath believed she had finally met her equal—someone who was smart, strong, creative, and passionate about writing—but the relationship was often volatile. They married after four months in a quiet ceremony and kept the marriage secret (Plath was worried she might lose her Fulbright if the marriage was discovered). The marriage was exceptionally literary from the get-go. Plath and Hughes settled into a routine of writing and reading each other's work. Much of the time, however, Hughes would write and Plath would act as his secretary, sending out his poetry. He even won an important poetry contest that he didn't know Plath entered on his behalf. However, Hughes did support Plath's writing goals and encouraged her to write. In this way, the two had a more equitable artistic partnership than most.

In the 1950s—even in progressive artistic circles—there was still a sense that men dominated the world of work. Mostly, women were relegated to a more domestic experience: providing support for their husband, taking care of the home, and raising the children. It might be seen as a bonus to have a clever wife who would write sometimes. But Plath bristled against losing her identity as a writer to household drudgery.

In 1957, Plath and Hughes moved to back to the United States to pursue jobs in education. They settled in Massachusetts, and Plath began teaching English at her alma mater, Smith College. Although she was regarded as a good professor, Plath felt that teaching took her away from achieving success as a writer. Both she and Hughes decided to dedicate themselves to writing from then on and only take jobs that could allow them to focus on that goal. At this time, Hughes' poetry collection *The Hawk in the Rain* had been well received by American poets, and Plath and Hughes were invited to mingle with Boston's literati.

Plath took two part-time jobs and began auditing classes in Boston taught by well-regarded and eccentric poet Robert Lowell. This class exposed Plath to yet another kind of writing: "confessional" poetry. Confessional poets like Lowell, John Berryman, and Allen Ginsberg wrote about their personal experiences in explicit terms, often breaking social taboos by writing about sexuality, trauma, or addiction in the first person. Lowell's poetic use of "I" blurred the lines between the writer and the speaker of the poem, inspiring Plath to continue playing with the relationship between art and personal experience. While taking Lowell's class, Plath met fellow poet Anne Sexton. Sexton, who had begun writing poetry after having a nervous breakdown, was flamboyant and open—and she was an important up-and-coming poet. Plath and Sexton became friendly and would go out for drinks at the Ritz to talk about poetry and about their struggles with mental illness. As we will explore further in Chapter 3, Sexton became an influence on Plath's poetry.

During this time, Plath was trying to figure out how to move forward in her life as a poet and also become a mother. In 1960, Plath discovered she was pregnant, and she and Hughes decided to move back to England and rent a London apartment. A big year of both successes and setbacks lay ahead. On February 10, 1960, Plath signed a contract for her first book of poetry: *The Colossus and Other Poems*. A few months later, Plath's daughter Frieda was born. Plath became pregnant again later in the year but had a miscarriage followed by appendicitis. In a letter to Dr. Beuscher, Plath explained that prior to the miscarriage, Hughes had hit her: "Ted beat me up physically a couple of days before my miscarriage: the baby I lost was due to be born on his birthday. I felt this an aberration, & felt I had given him some cause, I had torn some of his papers in half." Later, Plath would indicate that Hughes also verbally and emotionally abused her as their marriage became strained.

GROWING AS A WRITER

The Colossus and Other Poems received good reviews, but Plath wanted more success and a room of her own. While in recovery from appendicitis, Plath began to plan her first novel as well as write more poetry. By 1961, she was deep at work on *The Bell Jar*, mostly keeping this project a secret. She and Hughes moved out of London and into the country to a house called Court Green where they would have more space to write. This was a turbulent time in Plath's life but also one of unbridled creativity. Plath was very prolific while at

Court Green and somehow in between caring for her daughter, giving birth to her son, Nicholas, and finding out her husband was having an affair, she wrote with great urgency what would eventually become most of *Ariel* (1965), an extraordinary and genre-changing collection of poems that would make Plath famous after its posthumous publication.

With the end of her marriage looming, Plath returned to London with her children to start life as a single parent. In January 1963, *The Bell Jar* was published under the pseudonym Victoria Lucas to mostly positive reviews—but unfortunately Plath did not live to see most of them. Plath had ambitions for her novel but deferentially referred to it as a "potboiler"—meaning a sensationalistic or shocking book. That she chose to publish under a pen name has been interpreted by scholars as evidence that Plath was concerned readers who were familiar with her story (such as friends or family) would see the text as purely autobiographical, since it is the story of a young woman who attempts suicide after an internship at a prestigious women's magazine. Plath wrote to her brother that it was a "secret" and "no one must read it!" To be fair, most of the people written about in *The Bell Jar* do not appear in a positive light— although this adds to the book's unexpected comedic power.

The winter of 1963 in London was one of the coldest to date. Plath had been thrown by the dissolution of her marriage and the prospect of life without Ted. She was alone in a country where she did not have a strong support system. And she was parenting two small children in a freezing apartment where things kept breaking. Though her depression had returned with a vengeance, Plath fought to stay optimistic and productive, but it was too hard. Her letters during this time show a woman continually reaching out to all her support systems but feeling entirely overwhelmed and heartbroken: "What appals [sic] me is the return of my madness, my paralysis, my fear & vision of the worst—cowardly withdrawal, a mental hospital, lobotomies," she wrote to Dr. Beuscher (*Letters Vol. 2*, 2018, p. 967).

THE CREATION OF PLATH THE MYTH

Here's where Plath's life transforms into mythology, where a woman trying to survive the winter becomes a mad poet scribbling in the early morning poems of violence and otherworldliness. In this myth, Plath paces the small apartment twisting her hair. Her eyes are wild. She writes and writes and writes as if possessed. Her friend, writer and critic Al Alvarez, penned an iconic description that furthered this image:

I hardly recognised Sylvia when she opened the door. The bright young American house wife with her determined smile and crisp clothes had vanished along with the pancake make-up, the school-mistressy bun and fake cheerfulness. Her face was wax-pale and drained: her hair hung loose down to her waist and left a faint, sharp animal scent on the air when she walked ahead of me up the stairs. She looked like a priestess emptied out by the rites of her cult. And perhaps that is what she had become. She had broken through to whatever it was that made her want to write, the poems were coming every day, sometimes as many as three a day, unbidden, unstoppable, and she was off in a closed, private world where no one was going to follow her. (Alvarez, 1970)

In reality, we can never know what went through Sylvia Plath's mind during this time. Through letters she wrote and interviews with friends and neighbors during her last few weeks, we know Plath reached out to friends, her primary care physician, Dr. Horder, and her former therapist, Dr. Beuscher. Plath was severely depressed and without adequate support: "I am suddenly in agony, desperate, thinking Yes let him [Hughes] take over the house, the children, let me just die & be done with it. How can I get out of this ghastly defeatist cycle & grow up. I am only too aware that love and a husband are impossibles to me at this time, I am incapable of being myself and loving myself," she wrote to Beuscher on February 4.

On Monday, February 11, 1963, Plath died by suicide. She sealed herself off in the kitchen, away from her children, and turned the gas on. She left the manuscript for *Ariel and Other Poems* neatly on her desk. Later, Dr. Horder explained that he had found a bed for Plath at a mental hospital and she was set to be admitted on February 11 (Clark, 2020, p. 891). Biographer Heather Clark thinks that, in addition to suffering from depression and using medications carelessly, "the prospect of a potentially horrific stay in an unknown mental hospital was one that filled Plath with fear...she was on the verge of surrendering herself to unknown psychiatrists—likely all men—in a notorious asylum" (Clark, 2020, p. 887).

Plath did not leave a suicide letter; a note was found by the baby stroller that simply read: "PLEASE CALL DR. HORDER AT PRI 3804." Plath's body was discovered that morning by the visiting nurse she had enlisted to help care for the children.

Ariel and Other Poems was later edited by Ted Hughes and published as *Ariel* in 1965. In a controversial move, Hughes reorganized the structure of the manuscript and removed poems that he considered cast him in a bad light. Hughes chose to end *Ariel* on "Words," a poem that references fate in its last lines: "fixed stars govern a life." What Hughes seemed to be saying with his reorganization was that Plath's suicide was unpreventable and destined to happen—thus distancing himself from his wife's desperate act.

In 2004, Frieda Hughes released her mother's original poetic manuscript, which showed the public that her mother had a very different vision of the collection that made her famous. In particular, Plath concluded her version with the cycle of bee poems, with the last line of the last poem giving a sense of optimism: "The bees are flying. They taste the spring."

THE TROUBLE WITH BIOGRAPHY

One of the biggest issues in Plath studies has revolved around Plath's biography: Who gets to tell her story and what written version of this life do we trust? What are the biases? What is at stake? Especially when the person being written about is not alive, and therefore cannot defend herself, the issue of biography remains complicated to this day.

Biographies are intended to be factual accounts of a person's life. Using eyewitness accounts, interviews, and artifacts such as letters and journal entries, biographers do the best they can to craft a truthful portrait. But as we have learned over time, eyewitness accounts can be faulty. Memories can change or evolve. And as we see from the editorial controversy around *Ariel*, narratives can be molded to satisfy certain agendas depending on who is determining them.

When biographers initially started to tackle Plath's life, they came up against various roadblocks. The most difficult to get around was Ted Hughes and his sister Olwyn. Olwyn had been placed in charge of Plath's estate and controlled who was able to use and quote from Plath's work and access her private materials. Specifically, biographers who were inclined to treat her brother with a gentle touch tended to get permission. One biographer, Linda Wagner-Martin, explained as much in the Preface to *Sylvia Plath: A Life* (1987): "When I began researching this biography in 1982, I contacted Olwyn Hughes, who is literary executor of the Sylvia Plath estate. Olwyn was initially cooperative and helped me in my research . . . . As Olwyn read the later chapters of the book, however . . . her cooperation diminished" (Wagner-Martin, 1987, pp. 13–14). Wagner-Martin also added that both Olwyn and Ted's refusal to cooperate led to her inability to use more of Plath's writing in the book: "Consequently, this biography contains less of Plath's writing than I had intended. The alternative would have been to agree to suggestions that would have changed the point of view of this book appreciably" (Wagner-Martin, 1987, p. 14).

In 1996, Olwyn gave up control of the estate to Frieda and Nicholas. After Nicholas's suicide in 2009, the estate fell solely to Frieda. Currently, Faber & Faber assists Frieda with administrative duties. Having the estate under Frieda's control has made it much easier for biographers to use material, and for readers to learn more about Plath's life and work.

Because *Ariel* eventually became a foundational text in American literature, and because Sylvia's death became so tied to those poems, her work took on new meaning. But to look at all of Plath's literary products through the veil of her suicide would be to do the poems a disservice.

Plath is not defined by her death. She was a human being who experienced the highs and lows of life and created art inspired by everything from nature to love to childbirth to traveling and so much more. Too often, the poems that deal most directly with mental illness and suicide have been made to stand in for Plath's entire oeuvre, obscuring the range of her poetic interests. As Frieda writes, "I saw poems such as 'Lady Lazarus' and 'Daddy' dissected over and over, the moment that my mother wrote them being applied to her whole life, to her whole person, as if they were the total sum of her experience." Plath's death does not represent her entire life and work, but it is an example of how society can let down people who struggle with mental illness. Her art remains a testament to how someone with mental illness can still live a full and productive life.

Plath's life as well as her poetry and prose continue to influence readers in all kinds of ways. Plath is now a pop culture icon and a central figure in American literature. Whereas, when I was growing up and we studied one Plath poem, there are now entire college courses dedicated to Plath studies, indicating that her work is being taken more seriously. Conferences are held, books are written, and paintings and sculpture are created. Her London apartment at 3 Chalcot Square is a national landmark. People make journeys to her grave in Heptonstall, England, to leave pens. Her legacy is one of empowerment, especially for young women who feel stifled by societal expectations. When we study Sylvia Plath's life, we study all the ways that a woman was able to thrive, for a time, in a world that didn't expect her to achieve much.

Chapter 2
Plath in Her Historical Context

Plath came of age during a tumultuous period in American history—the 1940s and 1950s—and her understanding of the world affected how she saw herself as both a woman and a writer. It is vital, when reading Plath's work, to place it in the context in which it was written in order to discover all the layers and possible meanings. Doing so does not negate the universal beauty of poetry or literature as a self-contained work of art; rather, it adds new dimensions to our perspective. Understanding the background of a writer helps us more fully appreciate an artistic work and all its nuance, not to mention the elements that make it both timely and timeless.

COLD WAR CULTURE

Plath grew up during the end of World War II (1939–1945) and the beginning of the Cold War (1947–1991). Her childhood was defined by World War II and its aftermath—the liberation of Nazi death camps across Europe, the United States' detonation of two atomic bombs in Japan, and tension among world powers over potential nuclear domination. Plath learned about the Holocaust and the atomic bomb and grew up in an America anxious about Communism.

She was a high school student when the first phase of the Cold War began, and she died months after the Cuban Missile Crisis (1962) ushered in phase two.

The Cold War (1947–1991) was a period of tension between the United States and its allies and the then Soviet Union and its allies. The two nations struggled for dominance not on the battlefield but through propaganda campaigns, espionage, technological competitions such as the Space Race, and others.

Born in New England to a German immigrant father and second-generation Austrian mother, Plath felt conflicted about her German and Austrian heritage. In particular, Plath worried about whether or not her father had Nazi leanings. FBI files from 1918 show that Otto Plath was examined for being potentially sympathetic to the German cause. Apparently, Otto had been passed over for teaching positions at the University of California, and he considered himself "persecuted without just cause" because of his German background. However, there was no evidence for disloyalty. Otto Plath renounced his German and Polish citizenship in 1926 and became an American citizen. In the FBI files, Otto tells investigators that his parents came to the United States "because of the better conditions" but also defended his homeland: "Some things are rotten in Germany, but not all; that the German people and their character is not altogether rotten."

While Sylvia did not know any of this, it is possible that she could sense her father's anger—after all, he believed that his employers persecuted him due to his status as a German immigrant. Aurelia Schober Plath was also taunted for being of Austrian descent during the Great War; in the Introduction to *Letters Home,* she describes how she was bullied during her childhood: "Even though my father became an American citizen as soon as that privilege was possible, our name Schober, with its German sound, resulted in my being ostracized by the neighborhood 'gang,' called 'spy-face,' and at one time being pushed off the school bus steps and dumped on the ground, while the bus driver, keeping his eyes straight ahead, drove off" (*Letters Home,* 1975, p. 4). Like her mother, Plath's later attempts to conform to normative, American values and traditions may have stemmed from her childhood feelings of being an outsider.

Consequently, Plath's identity as the daughter of a German immigrant influenced her sense of self as well as her poetry. As biographer Heather Clark explains, Plath's German and Austrian identity "helps explain this . . . hard-driving, intense immigrant work ethic that Plath in some ways inherited."

In other words, because Plath was the child of an immigrant—and an immigrant whose country of birth had done inexcusable, atrocious things—she must have felt like she had to work twice as hard, both to succeed and to also prove her Americanness.

From Plath's journals and letters, Plath's political identity seemed formed early on. She was an avowed pacifist and critical of American exceptionalism (for example, she did not understand why America and only America should have control of nuclear weapons). She also criticized the Korean War (1950–1953), saying it was neither "brave or heroic" and explained that she believed the fight against Communism was foolish: "That word, Communism, is blinding. No one knows exactly what it means, and yet they hate everything associated with it."

During the 1950s, Americans endured an age of suspicion and scrutiny. Everyone was watching everyone else—a byproduct of national obsession with surveillance regarding Communism. Critic Deborah Nelson explains how "in the late 1950s and early 1960s, the period when Plath was writing her last and best work, alarms over the loss of privacy were being raised in relation to the suburbs, television, the computer, psychoanalysis, the FBI and the police, record keeping in institutions . . . new technologies of surveillance . . . tabloid journalism, photojournalism and more" (Nelson, 2002, p. 31). When Senator Joseph McCarthy, who became most associated with unethical searches for communists, visited Smith College to give a lecture on the "Red Terror" Plath stood up and hissed at him alongside several classmates and professors (Winder, 2013, p. 147).

In his allegorical play *The Crucible* (1952/53), American playwright Arthur Miller equated the 1692 Salem Witch Trials to the McCarthyist witch-hunt for communists during the 1950s. At this time, heresy and finger-pointing were enough to get an individual blacklisted or even killed without any evidence. The House Committee on Un-American Activities began targeting Hollywood production companies and actors for reported subversive behaviors, and some artists, though never proven "guilty" of communist sympathies, never recovered their careers. For Miller, just as seventeenth-century Salem was an age of mass hysteria, so was Cold War America. Those on the outskirts—minority figures—were most susceptible.

We know that even as a straight, white woman, Plath felt watched. In an environment in which *conformity culture* ruled, she worried about being considered an outsider and was anxious about her appearance. Her mental health struggles branded her as someone living with a disability, although Plath would have probably not considered herself disabled in the way we now consider mental illness an invisible disability.

Conformity culture is when a society is defined by a sense of uniformity and rigidity that pervades all aspects of life. In a conformity culture, stability is prized over questioning established norms and thinking critically and independently.

GENDER AND SEXUALITY

Plath had beliefs about sex and gender that were feminist-forward and liberal. Moreover, she struggled to assert herself as an artist during a time when women were expected to support men and even sacrifice their ambitions in support of a *heteronormative*, family-focused existence. Consider that when Plath was born, American women had only been allowed to vote for twelve years. Additionally, women were largely discouraged from working in professions such as medicine, law, higher education, and business. They were to be supporting players contained within the domestic sphere, making life easier for their working husbands by cooking, cleaning, and raising children. Today, over 100 years after the passage of the 19th Amendment giving women the right to vote, this might sound like a stereotype; nevertheless, for a vast majority of women in Plath's era, the 1950s was not a time to strike out into the world.

Heteronormativity is a worldview that promotes heterosexuality as the normal, default, or preferred sexual orientation.

Plath was ahead of her time—but she was also a product of her time. She was invested in her appearance and in maintaining a facade of perfection, but she also railed against the conformity culture of her day, actively pursuing a lifestyle that was unconventional by putting her art at the forefront. To do so required enormous courage and self-confidence, as the mixed messages women received during the 1950s (and still receive today) would be enough to turn any intelligent woman on her head: be attractive but not sexy, smart but not smarter than a man, demure but not a doormat, social but not too friendly, maternal but not homely, thrilling but not wild.

These mixed messages were partly the result of the role shift following the end of WW II, when women who had been working in male roles during the war were suddenly expected to return to their domestic roles in the home. Women had proven themselves capable—emotionally, mentally, and physically. Far from the supposed "weaker sex," American women had made themselves valuable contributors to the war. Think of the popularized image of Rosie the Riveter, with her feminine head scarf, flexed muscle, and can-do facial expression.

While white, middle-class women enjoyed more rights and privileges than they had previously, they were still trapped by a system that encouraged them to pursue a domestic life. College might be a fun diversion while you were looking for a husband. Sexual double standards ruled the day; men were allowed to engage in sex before marriage but women were not. Sexual assault was not treated seriously, and women were often blamed for bringing unwanted sexual attention to themselves by the way they acted or dressed. Pregnancy outside of marriage loomed large as a threat. Reputations were ruined with gossip about "loose" behavior. Knowledge about contraception was limited and access to birth control even more so. Here is a quote from an anonymous 1950s sixteen-year-old who found herself abandoned and pregnant: "How are you supposed to know what they want? You hold out for a long time and then when you do give in to them and give your body they laugh at you afterwards and say they'd never marry a slut. . ." (D'Emilio and Freedman, 1988, p. 262).

If Plath already felt herself caught in the crosshairs of her American identity and German ancestry, she also grew up in an era of gender paradoxes that further complicated her vision of self and society alike: "Although proud, self-respecting women of lower socioeconomic status would remain in the workforce out of necessity, Sylvia Plath . . . entered adulthood at a moment that was peculiarly hostile to career-oriented, white, educated women" (Harding, 2019, p. 180). The "nuclear family," which referred to a heterosexual married couple with children, was the standard during this time. Family was the focus, with fairly strict gender lines drawn regarding roles.

If you've ever watched TV programs from the 1950s such as *Leave It to Beaver* (1957–1963) or *The Donna Reed Show* (1958–1966), you may be familiar with cultural icons like June Cleaver. Such TV programs helped reinforce the binary roles of men as workers outside the home and of women—vacuuming in their pearls and high heels, with nary a hair out of place—as workers within the domestic sphere. Is it any wonder that this was also the era of the Barbie Doll (first manufactured in 1959) with her unrealistic feminine figure?

During the 1955 commencement exercises at Smith College—the year Plath graduated—Democratic presidential candidate Adlai Stevenson gave a speech to the graduating class: "Many women feel frustrated and far apart from the great issues and stirring debates for which their education has given them understanding and relish. There is, often, a sense of contraction, of closing horizons and lost opportunities. They had hoped to play their part in the crisis of the age. But what they do is wash the diapers."

In her work, Plath taps into this sense of frustration and futility: Here are some of the best and brightest young women America has to offer, but their potential is ignored in favor of upholding patriarchal hegemony. Continuously, women were being told to either become a wife and mother and give up their aspirations or choose to pursue a life of the mind and end up a spinster. It may sound reductive now, but many young women during the 1950s were faced with what seemed like this impossible decision.

In her journals, Plath vacillates between rebelling against this vision and accepting it. She writes about longing to escape a life in which she feels doomed to marry a man who would "worship woman as a sex machine with rounded breasts and a convenient opening in the vagina, as a painted doll who shouldn't have a thought in her pretty head other than cooking a steak dinner" (*Unabridged Journals*, 2000, p. 36). Two years later, she weighs the pros and cons of married life a bit differently: "I am learning how to compromise the wild dream ideals and the necessary realities without such screaming pain. . . . I believe I could paint, write, and keep a home and husband too. . . . I could be more of a prisoner as an older, tense, cynical career girl than as a richly creative wife and mother who is always growing intellectually" (*Unabridged Journals*, 2000, p. 164).

MENTAL HEALTH

The 1950s were a time of great strides in mental healthcare—and yet, looking back, it all seems terribly crude. A few significant advances were the popularization of Sigmund Freud's psychoanalytic theories, introduction of Thorazine (chlorpromazine), electroconvulsive therapy, and the burgeoning antipsychiatry movement. Much of what was pushing the mental health field to advance was the number of WW II veterans returning home from battle with post-traumatic stress disorder, then called "combat stress reaction." People were more open about mental health struggles, and in some cases (wealthy, white families), it was even seen as glamorous to have a Freudian analyst—it meant you were worldly and complex (Pfister, 1997, p. 171). Still, there was a great deal of stigma, and people who suffered from mental illness often felt deep shame that they could not will themselves out of their state.

In 1954, chlorpromazine, an antipsychotic drug, was licensed by the U.S. Food and Drug Administration. It was initially intended to treat patients suffering from schizophrenia—and in some cases, it helped— but soon it was being prescribed for a shocking number of problems. For example, advertisements for Thorazine announced that the drug could be used for everything from senility to menopause to depression to alcoholism. Side effects could include drowsiness, dry mouth, and tardive dyskinesia, which is a disorder involving involuntary movements. A lot of the popular images of psychiatric patients refer back to chlorpromazine patients shuffling around, more like zombies than people.

Electroconvulsive therapy (ECT) was first used in 1938. The therapy became popular in the United States in the 1940s at a time when psychiatric hospitals were over-crowded with long-term or chronic patients. When given properly, ECT can help treatment resistant depression and other issues. It is still widely used today but with more refinement than the past, such as the inclusion of anesthesia (Shorter and Healy, 2007, p. 3).

Plath was a recipient of botched and therapeutic ECT, which deeply traumatized her and pervaded her writing. As a woman, Plath had no agency over her medical treatment; "She was at the mercy of a patriarchal medical system that assumed that highly ambitious, strong-willed women were neurotic" (Clark, 2020, p. 271). Some of Plath's most notable moments in *The Bell Jar* involve scenes revolving around mental health experiences. During her first visit with her psychiatrist Dr. Gordon, protagonist Esther Greenwood is hopeless about this man's ability to help her. Dr. Gordon makes sexist comments and questions whether Esther's illness is real or not. "Suppose you try and tell me what you think is wrong?" he asks Esther, implying that her depressive episode is some kind of exaggerated event. She understands as much, saying to herself, "That made it sound as if nothing was *really* wrong, I only *thought* it was wrong." Later, Dr. Gordon administers botched ECT that traumatizes Esther and leads to her suicide attempt.

After her suicide attempt and during her hospitalization at McLean, Plath received ECT again despite her misgivings and fear, but it was administered correctly and with care. The ECT was considered successful, as Plath reentered society and resumed her studies. However, Plath hated the treatment even when administered correctly. Though she did improve in the short term, "her chief complaint was the recovery period after each treatment, during which she felt keenly her loss of identity" (Clark, 2020, p. 297). For the rest of her life, Plath would worry about relapsing and having to receive more ECT.

The stigma associated with mental illness during the 1950s (and even, unfortunately, now) was very real to Plath. She would do whatever she could to convince the world, after her suicide attempt and hospitalization, that she was "normal." For Plath, ideas about mental health were inextricably linked to ideas about physical appearance and identity. Plath's writing about the female body is a way to see how deeply this cultural moment affected her understanding of the self and the body. Plath's struggles with chronic, often repulsive sinusitis, the displeasing plumpness of her nose, the scar on her cheek from her 1953 suicide attempt, as well as her posture and "expressionless eyes" (*Unabridged Journals,* 2000, p. 155) are all documented with frequency in her journals and letters and transformed in literary works. Her preoccupation with appearance, bodily functions, and disability can be connected to contemporary notions of health and wellness as well as femininity (Grisafi, 2016).

Critics such as Sally Bayley have noted that Plath was a very visual person as well as a consumer of popular media images such as those in magazines. She read self-help articles and beauty advice. The issue of *Mademoiselle* that was produced during Plath's internship included a self-help article that emphasized: "the female potential for visual transformation . . . the advice given implies that psychological problems can be remedied by the ability of the female to transform her physical self. Indeed, her physical self is both her redemption and her cure" (Bayley, 2007, p. 196). What is endearingly known in Plath circles as "the platinum summer" illustrates the logic behind this kind of "help." After her suicide attempt, "Plath dyed her hair a shocking shade of blonde, a move intended to distract others from the fact that her body wore the ravages of her psychiatric ordeal—a prominent scar under her eye from an injury sustained in the crawl space and a constant reminder and marker of suicide attempt" (Grisafi, 2016). Such is an example of conformity through beauty, concealing "evidence" of a past suicide attempt.

By the 1960s, psychopharmacology was becoming a more popular type of therapy for mental illness. Medication intended to treat depression, schizophrenia, anxiety, and other disorders became more widely prescribed both for in-patient and out-patient treatment. Although medical professionals were optimistic about the new strides in psychopharmacology, it was (and still is) difficult to predict how a patient would respond to medication. When Plath died, she had just begun taking an antidepressant; it is possible that she experienced suicidal feelings as a side-effect of starting this medication.

In the late 1950s, there were some professionals within the psychiatric community who were critical of the increase of medication administration to those suffering from mental illness. Called the antipsychiatry movement, these doctors and therapists were concerned about the unequal power dynamics between doctor and patient, the trampling of constitutional rights and free will, and the possibility of a world filled with people who were medicated for what could be called problems with everyday life. Society was messed up, not the person, stressed the antipsychiatry proponent.

Today, we know that mental health is more complex than either "medicate everyone" or "flush your pills down the toilet and be free." We understand that sometimes certain medications can be overprescribed. We also know that many people benefit greatly from psychiatric medication. Plath's writing comes from the perspective of someone who was both failed and helped by psychiatry. *The Bell Jar* certainly traffics in antipsychiatry rhetoric, but is not as obviously critical as other works like Ken Kesey's *One Flew Over the Cuckoo's Nest* (1962).

ON THE EVE OF SECOND WAVE FEMINISM

Plath died in February 1963—right when the second wave of feminism was beginning to coalesce with the publication of Betty Friedan's *The Feminine Mystique*, which was published eight days after Plath's death. If Plath had lived, she would have seen many of her anxieties addressed by a strong, feminist collective that sought to bring about practical changes in women's lives. With its emphasis on sexual liberation, financial and personal autonomy, and pursuing goals outside of the home such as a career, art, or community organizing, feminism's second wave attempted to solve what Betty Friedan called "the problem that has no name": widespread depression among housewives who felt their lives were degrading and they had no identity.

The second wave of feminism addressed many of the issues related to the cult of domesticity that thrived post World War II, including women's work, birth control, family dynamics, and participation in politics. It brought about legal victories such as the Equal Pay Act of 1963, Title VII of the Civil Rights Act of 1964 (prohibiting employment discrimination based on race, color, religion, sex, and national origin), and the *Griswold v. Connecticut* Supreme Court ruling of 1965 (which determined that a ban on contraceptive use violated the right to marital privacy). In 1966, Friedan and others formed the National Organization for Women (NOW).

In the wake of renewed work to secure women's rights, Plath's legacy was co-opted, her story told as a cautionary tale of the perils of being a woman during the 1950s (Badia, 2006, p. 131). She was seen as ahead of her time, an astute observer of sexism and female rage and sorrow. There was anger toward Ted Hughes, who was seen as killing a genius. Fans of Plath's work and those emotionally touched by her story saw Hughes as a cruel man who abandoned Plath and their children. For them, he represented the patriarchy and a long history of men who tried to silence or twist the words of women. Plath became a feminist symbol, and, even now, her work can be read as a feminist battle cry.

Chapter 3
Plath's Poetry

INTRODUCTION TO THE POEMS

Before Plath ended up on T-shirts and references in blockbuster movies, there were the poems. "In these poems, written in the last months of her life and often rushed out at the rate of two or three a day, Sylvia Plath becomes herself, becomes something imaginary, newly, wildly and subtly created," poet Robert Lowell wrote in the Foreword to *Ariel*. Lowell may have been helping promote himself a bit—Plath was a student of his—but the fervor over *Ariel* was real. While Lowell's Foreword helped establish the myth of Sylvia Plath, the work always stood on its own.

Initially, Plath's reputation rested on *Ariel*. This was the volume that catapulted her to posthumous fame as well as secured her a place in American literature. But *Ariel* did not magically appear. Plath had been writing poetry since she was young, absorbing the world around her and evolving as a person and an artist. She worked for years on her poetic craft, read widely, took workshops, and shared her poetry with others for criticism. She pondered the events of her historical moment and worked on creative ways to express her anxieties about a world seemingly on the brink of war.

While Plath considered herself political and wrote political poetry, she is most often considered a poet who mined life for inspiration. She certainly used her life as a creative source, but we have to be careful not to conflate Plath the writer with the speaker of her poems and the protagonist of her fiction. These two entities are always different. Poems are not journals; they are art objects that use language as a medium to convey larger truths about the world.

In poetry, an event from someone's personal experience can be transformed into a larger statement about our culture or more universal events. This is not to disparage autobiography—which is a useful medium in its own right and a traditional form used by otherwise marginalized voices—but to emphasize the crucial differences.

PLATH'S INFLUENCES

While Plath was influenced by the world around her, she was also a student of poetry and read widely. In her early work, we can see her trying out different styles based on whom she was reading at the time. Writers like Dylan Thomas, W.B. Yeats, W.H. Auden, T.S. Eliot, Wallace Stevens, Theodore Roethke, and D.H. Lawrence were great influences on Plath's work. Plath even attempted to meet Dylan Thomas (considered something of a rock star in the poetry world, always drunk and the center of attention) in New York City, but it didn't work out. Instead, as Plath's friend Carol recalls, the two of them sat outside Thomas's room at the famously bohemian Chelsea Hotel for the entire night—but Thomas did not show up (Winder, 2013, p. 185).

Plath was also influenced by philosophers and psychologists. She read Friedrich Nietzsche, Sigmund Freud, and Erich Fromm; though Plath was not very religious (she was a casual Unitarian), she was spiritual and interested in religious ritual, the occult, astrology, and other esoteric topics. References to magic, tarot cards, spirits, and witchcraft populate her poetry.

But one of the biggest literary influences on Plath was her own husband, Ted Hughes. Even before Hughes was Plath's husband, he was a poet she admired. Plath was inspired by Hughes's precise use of language, his bold and violent imagery, and his references to the natural world of animals and the animalistic impulses of humanity. This is because Plath was also interested in those concerns. Hughes's poetry was not polite, and Plath disdained artifice. She was always fighting to get to the difficult truth of the poem: "The kind of toughness and knottiness that we admire, both of us. . .perhaps that's why we met in the first place because we both felt we had similar interests," Plath said of their poetic relationship in a 1961 interview with the British Broadcasting Company (BBC).

Plath was influenced by Hughes's work, but she also approached the relationship from the perspective of an already published poet with her own goals and interests. The truth is, Plath and Hughes both borrowed from each other, and the relationship was mutually beneficial for both—for a time

Figure 3.1 Sylvia Plath and Ted Hughes on their honeymoon, 1956.
Source: CSU Archives / Everett Collection / Adobe Stock

(Clark, 2011, p. 19). For example, Hughes's poem "Full Moon and Little Frieda" borrows language from Plath's "Morning Song"—and both poems are about the birth of a child (Middlebrook, 2003, p. 162). Diane Middlebrook characterizes Plath and Hughes's poetic relationship as one of "call and response," which means that their work was in a constant poetic conversation.

In 1962, Plath explained that she was very interested in a new kind of "personal" poetry: confessional poetry. "I've been very excited by what I feel is the new breakthrough that came with, say, Robert Lowell's *Life Studies*, this intense breakthrough into very serious, very personal, emotional experience which I feel has been partly taboo," Plath said in an interview with Peter Orr of The British Council. "Robert Lowell's poems about his experience in a mental hospital, for example, interested me very much," Plath shared. "I think that personal experience is very important, but certainly it shouldn't be a kind of shut-box and mirror looking, narcissistic experience. I believe it should be relevant, and relevant to the larger things, the bigger things such as Hiroshima and [the concentration camp] Dachau and so on." This kind of melding of the personal and the political was a new poetic endeavor, and at the time it was quite revolutionary. Her statement about narcissism shows that Plath was aware of the criticisms launched at confessional poetry at the time and that she disagreed with them; her statement shows she believed it was possible to draw connections between global events and private lives.

As a genre, *confessional poetry* is loosely defined as poetry that emerged in the United States during the late 1950s and early 1960s that focuses on the "I" or first-person speaker of the poem. Confessional poems mostly deal with very personal experiences such as trauma, mental illness, death, sexuality, and motherhood and parenting. These experiences are often set in conversation with broader social or political themes. The most well-known confessional poets are Robert Lowell, Anne Sexton, John Berryman, W.D. Snodgrass, and Sylvia Plath.

Lowell wasn't the only confessional poet Plath admired; she had a friendship and working relationship with Anne Sexton: "I think particularly the poetess Anne Sexton, who writes about her experiences as a mother, as a mother who has had a nervous breakdown, is an extremely emotional and feeling young woman and her poems are wonderfully craftsman-like poems and yet they have a kind of emotional and psychological depth which I think is something perhaps quite new, quote exciting," Plath said in the Orr interview.

Plath gravitated to Sexton, and the two maintained a friendship over the years, with Plath arguably influenced by Sexton to be more daring with her work. Early in 1962, Anne Sexton sent Plath a copy of her successful and popular poetry collection *All My Pretty Ones*—which had been getting much more attention than Plath's work. "Critical acclaim for Sexton's work may well have prompted Plath to take risks in her poetry" (Bundtzen, 2001, p. 64). What were those risks? More references to the stuff of mundane, everyday life and deeper exploration of her mental states—no matter how dark or disturbing.

The popularity of autobiography had a lot to do with the turn toward confessional poetry, suggests Deborah Nelson. "The broader turn towards autobiography in literature, of which confessional poetry is one part, constituted one of the most visible ways that post-World War II writing differed from modernist writing. Personal voice, which materialized not only in every literary form, but also in the fine arts, mass culture, and politics, has been understood as an effect of new social forces like psychotherapy and mass celebrity as well as a lingering manifestation of American religious devotion" (Nelson, 2002, p. 22). The difference between autobiography and confessional poetry, though, lies in confessional poetry's ambiguity, by its ability to be molded and transformed, to blur the lines between the speaker and the poet.

Confessional poetry can be confusing because it offers the reader a sense of intimacy that might actually be artifice. There's an art in creating an atmosphere as shifting and unstable as the mind itself. Writing confessional poetry isn't scrawling in a diary; as with every other kind of poetry, the poet is concerned about form, craftsmanship, and tone. There is also much revision. The idea that confessional poems just "happen" and writers don't work or rework them, merely writing in a stream-of-conscious manner, is wrong. The poems may feel spontaneous, but that's part of the aesthetic. Spending time in the archives, an individual can see just how much Plath worked on perfecting her poems down to tiny line changes and even punctuation—she's infuriatingly meticulous, actually.

POETRY AS POLITICS

Today, considering the ubiquity of social media, we might talk about how privacy is a fiction. Nevertheless, during Plath's time, people were already having conversations about the loss of privacy. These discussions about privacy revolved around new spy technology and issues of surveillance in the political consciousness (Nelson, 2002, p. 75). Everyday Americans were concerned they were potentially being spied on by both the Communists and their own government—and they went above and beyond to make sure that they didn't look suspicious or subversive.

The time during which Plath lived is often referred to as the "Tranquilized Fifties" (from a poem by Robert Lowell). This name refers to the predominant cultural shift toward conformity culture and consumerism (and perhaps a reference to all the sedatives folks were taking behind the façade of happy homemaking). Everything appeared perfect on the surface, but writers like Plath wanted to get beneath the shiny, happy, grotesque masquerade to find the rot at the core and expose it. Plath's poems highlight the restrictions placed on women during the late 1950s and early 1960s and illustrate the damaging repercussions on a woman's sense of self.

Along with conformity culture and consumerism came more regressive politics. Spies and Communists could be anywhere, and the government leaned into paranoia. The Red Scare was in full effect in America, as Senator Joseph McCarthy and the House Committee on Un-American Activities were focused on rooting out Communists or Communist sympathizers, getting them blacklisted from work, and otherwise trampling their lives and civil liberties. So it only seems logical that writers would concern themselves with issues of privacy during this historical moment, an era of "McCarthyism" as it was called, where the home was considered sacred and outsiders were to be treated with suspicion. As critics have noted, confessional poetry is one way to regain control of one's privacy by deciding just how much to tell and how much to conceal (Nelson, 2002, p. 89). As Plath leaned more toward confessional poetics, she wrote more about issues that were seen as taboo.

The myth of Sylvia Plath would have you believe she just woke up one day and wrote the poems that made her famous. That's exciting and dramatic, but it's also not reality. Plath was a hard worker, a keen student, an observant human, and an engaged citizen. She was a perpetual learner, always seeking mentors and fellow writers. She kept her writing rejection slips, explaining that they showed she tried. Her life experiences formed the backbone of her poems, but the way she expressed those experiences is what makes them poetry. When we study Plath's poems, we see the evolution of certain themes and imagery as well as the choices she makes with language, line breaks, punctuation, and rhythm. This helps us understand Plath's poetic goals and how her poems relate to larger cultural issues during her time as well as continue to relate to ongoing issues in our own.

RECURRING THEMES IN PLATH'S WORK

Over the course of Plath's career, she wrote hundreds of poems. These poems sometimes deal with similar issues, demonstrating how Plath's conception of certain themes evolved over time. I include some of the themes that Plath revisits in her work, but this is in no way an exhaustive list. Additionally, multiple themes can exist in the same poem. As you read Plath's work, it's helpful to identify the themes and then explore how Plath uses tone, imagery, and form in conjunction with these themes to convey a message. Themes that turn up in Plath's poetry turn up in her fiction, essays, letters, and journals as well.

Bees and Beekeeping

Plath's father Otto was an expert on bees. He taught classes in entomology and authored a classic text called *Bumblebees and Their Ways.* Later in her life, Plath began beekeeping as a way of maintaining contact with her father's memory and fulfilling his legacy. She also enjoyed learning what she considered practical skills and had great plans to sell her own honey.

In her poems, Plath draws parallels between her father's power over bees and her own artistic power as a writer. In beekeeping, there is a formality to the process of gathering honey and tending to bees, and Plath sees the keeper of the bees as a kind of god. She makes connections between beekeeping and creativity, aligning the beekeeper and the writer and suggesting they both possess a special power: the ability to deal with and harness dangerous things.

In particular, critics have also interpreted Plath's bee poems as an affirmation of the creative, female self. Bee hives are a matriarchy and female bees are in charge! There is a queen in control and all the worker bees are female—and they are mostly all her offspring. In "Stings," Plath's speaker identifies with the queen bee, explaining "They thought death was worth it, but I/ have a self to recover, a queen."

In the bee cycle, which consists of "The Bee Meeting," "The Arrival of the Bee Box," "Stings," and "Wintering," Plath takes the reader on a journey from fear and alienation to eventual hope for a sweet future. "Wintering" was originally intended to be the last poem in *Ariel*, ending the collection on a note of optimism: "The bees are flying. They taste the spring." However, Ted Hughes reorganized the order of poems in that collection, putting the bee cycle toward the middle.

Domesticity

Plath felt pressure to participate in the 1950s culture. As a white, middle-class woman in her twenties, she was supposed to focus on getting married and having children. It was unusual for a woman to make her living entirely by a writing career. Plath also railed against what is called the "sexual double standard"—she felt that it was unfair men were able to be sexually active and have many partners when women were expected to be celibate until marriage.

Growing up, Plath wanted to transcend these stifling dictates and "have it all"—a career as a writer, the opportunity to have sexual experiences, and a marriage with someone she considered an equal. For Plath, the domestic space of the home functions as a symbol for confinement and oppression. In *The Bell Jar*, the home is written about with bitterness and disgust; it is a death trap, the place where feminine creativity is squashed. During the breakup of her marriage, Plath wrote to her mother that she was writing "terrific stuff, as if domesticity had choked me" (*Letters Vol. 2*, 2018, p. 856).

In Plath's poems such as "Letter in November" and "Lesbos," this conflict is apparent. In "Letter in November," Plath's speaker surveys her country property with pride: "I am so stupidly happy./My Wellingtons/Squelching and squelching through the beautiful red." In "Lesbos," the speaker provides an account of an unpleasant domestic visit. "Meanwhile there's a stink of fat and baby crap./I'm doped and thick from my last sleeping pill./The smog of cooking, the smog of hell," the speaker says acidly. These two extremes existed for Plath, making it all the more vital to consider the role that the 1950s cult of domesticity played in her work and her life.

Flowers

While flowers are a common symbol of love or happiness in poetry, for Plath, flowers take on a darker meaning. In Plath's work, flowers often symbolize jealousy or a conflict within the self—the speakers of Plath's flower poems are envious of how alive and vibrant flowers are, how colorful and carefree. Modernist poet T.S. Eliot's influence can be seen here, if we think of the first lines of his poem "The Waste Land": "April is the cruelest month, breeding/lilacs." There is a cruelty in watching nature continue to flourish indifferently while humankind suffers.

In Plath's poem "Tulips," the cut flowers in the speaker's sterile hospital room represent an unwelcome intrusion of life; the tulips remind a speaker content with dying that there is strength inside her if she cares to try. "I didn't want any flowers, I only wanted/To lie with my hands turned up and be utterly empty," the speaker protests, finding that the bright red tulips have invaded her death-like peace with their "loud noise." Similarly, in "Poppies in July," the speaker is exhausted watching the poppies "flickering" and wishes she could have their "opiates" to dull her pain.

Flowers are also associated with femininity and domesticity. In the poem "Fever 103°," Plath writes about flowers that require a lot of care and are unable to survive and thrive outside. In particular, she writes about hothouse orchids, referring to the common use of "hothouse flower" as a metaphor for a person who is fragile and sheltered. A "hothouse" flower must be tended to, as it is not strong enough to grow outside the greenhouse. For Plath, women can be considered hothouse flowers because they are sheltered and not allowed to face the elements and become strong.

The Holocaust

Though Plath didn't write many poems about the Holocaust, the ones that exist continue to be controversial. Plath's use of the Holocaust as a metaphor for personal suffering is a point of contention, with critics arguing about whether Plath's use of the Holocaust is ethical or not. At best, Plath's treatment of the Holocaust in her poetry can be seen as her "sense of connection with the events, and her desire to combine the public and the personal" (Strange-ways, 1997, p. 376). Similarly, her alignment with the Jewish people can be read as a way of exploring her feelings of alienation and issues of an identity against the backdrop of contemporary tragedy. At worst, it can be seen as exploitative and narcissistic.

As an American student, Plath learned about the Holocaust in high school and college, but her German and Austrian ancestry made her take a very personal approach to thinking through the atrocities Nazis inflicted on the Jewish population. Alongside her empathy with the Jewish community, Plath worried that her father might have had fascist leanings and sympathized with the Nazi party. In poems like "Daddy," Plath sets up a relationship between a Nazi father and a speaker who identifies with Jewish victims of the Holocaust. The poem is filled with references to Germany and the Holocaust such as the death camps, the Luftwaffe, swastikas, and Adolf Hitler's manifesto *Mein Kampf*. She even includes German words, illustrating the speaker's conflict with her father's native language.

Mental Health

Plath writes about depression and mental illness frequently in her poetry, but in *The Bell Jar* she extends her criticisms to the mental health institution and doctors. Mental illness is seen as symptomatic of the dark side of 1950s conformity culture. As a young woman coming of age during the Cold War, Plath felt oppressed by traditional cultural expectations. She saw mental health as possible only in a world where women were free to create and express themselves sexually. In *The Bell Jar*, male doctors are depicted as upholding patriarchal standards and not being especially good listeners. When Esther visits her first doctor, Dr. Gordon, he dismisses her concerns and ultimately gives her botched electroshock therapy that leads to her suicide attempt. While Esther is recovering at the hospital, the female Dr. Nolan provides Esther with helpful therapy. As a woman, she seems to understand Esther's problems and also helps Esther take control of her reproductive health by providing her with birth control.

In Plath's poetry, depression and suicide are also explored often in conjunction with the sea, flowers, birthdays, infidelity, and mythology. One of Plath's more famous poems, "Lady Lazarus," refers to the Biblical story of a man who rose from the dead. However, Plath rewrites the story to focus on what she sees as the spectacle of the suicide survivor. The poem takes on a flippant attitude toward suicide as a creative endeavor and type of rebirth: "Dying/Is an art, like everything else./I do it exceptionally well," the speaker brags, promoting her self-destructive tendencies as a talent. In other poems such as "Tulips" and "The Moon and the Yew Tree," Plath uses nature to explore depression and suicidal ideation, the desire for "blackness and silence."

Motherhood

"I want books and babies and beef stews," Plath wrote in her journals, illustrating her desire to integrate her literary ambitions with her domestic life. As a mother of two, Plath loved parenting; it gave her a sense of pride. She doted on her children and did her best to secure their futures. The poetry she writes about her children is incredibly moving and powerful, showing the strong links between creating new life and creating poetry. For example, after her separation from Ted Hughes, Plath wrote about parenting as a single mother and imagined how her youngest child Nicholas would feel now that his father was more absent in his life: "You will be aware of an absence, presently,/Growing beside you, like a tree," she writes in "For a Fatherless Son." In the same poem, she tries to find strength in the situation, "But right now you are dumb./And I love your stupidity."

It might not seem revolutionary, but writing about the struggles of motherhood—even motherhood at all—was bold. Motherhood was not seen as the stuff of poetry; it was too boring, too everyday. No one wanted to read poems about changing diapers—but that was changing with the Confessional movement and poets like Anne Sexton. After Plath had her daughter, Frieda, her perspective on motherhood changed significantly: "Motherhood produced a momentous, surprising effect in Plath's art. It extricated her imagination from the overwhelming influence of Ted Hughes, investing it in the instinctual processes of being female" (Middlebrook, 2003, p. 153).

Figure 3.2 Sylvia Plath and her mother, Aurelia Plath, with Plath's children, Frieda and Nicholas, in Devon, England, 1962.
Source: CSU Archives / Everett Collection / Adobe Stock

But Plath didn't always write about motherhood in a positive light. Motherhood is eviscerated in *The Bell Jar*, with all the mothers portrayed as idiots, victims, and baby machines. Esther sees her mother as pathetic, her neighbor Dodo with six children as grotesque, and her boyfriend's mother as absurd. "Children made me sick," Esther says. The threat of pregnancy prevents Esther from becoming sexually active, and she resents that men do not have to worry about becoming pregnant and being held responsible for raising the child. At this point in her life, for Esther, a baby would ruin all her hopes and dreams for the future. She sees pregnancy and childbirth as ways the patriarchy keeps women under control: "Maybe it was true that when you were married and had children it was like being brainwashed, and afterward you went about numb as a slave in some private, totalitarian state" (*The Bell Jar*, p. 69).

Nuclear War

Like Plath's references to the Holocaust in her work, critics have had to contend with her poetic use of nuclear war and the detonation of the atomic bombs on the Japanese cities of Hiroshima and Nagasaki. It's clear that these events of World War II had a profound influence on how Plath saw the world;

she considered herself a pacifist and was scared of fascist violence. She wrote about her fears of nuclear attack even as a young woman, journaling: "They're really going to mash up the world this time, the damn fools. When I read that description of the victims of Nagasaki I was sick: 'And we saw that first looked like lizards crawling up the hill, croaking. It got lighter and we could see that it was humans, their skin burned off, and their bodies broken where they had been thrown against something.' Sounds like something out of a horror story. God save us from doing that again" (*Unabridged Journals,* 2000, p. 46).

After Plath gave birth to Frieda, she brought the baby to a "Ban the Bomb" event at Trafalgar Square, telling her mother, "I felt proud that the baby's first real adventure should be as a protest against the insanity of world-annihilation—already a certain percentage of unborn children are doomed by fallout & noone [sic] knows the cumulative effects of what is already poisoning the air & sea" (*Letters Vol. 2,* 2018, p. 462).

Tracy Brain has noted that the imagery of a burning or too-hot sun appears in some of Plath's poems, and she considers this a direct reference to nuclear radiation or something environmentally unnatural (Brain, 2001, p. 107). But the poem that most fully uses nuclear war as a central theme is "Fever 103°" Written in 1962, the poem details the suffering of a speaker with a rising temperature but makes references to nuclear blasts, thus once again combining the personal with the political. The fever seems to be both painful and purifying for the speaker, and as the fever rages on, she gets closer and closer to self-annihilation: "My selves dissolving," the speaker says. With references to smoke, radiation, and "Hiroshima ash," the poem explores how the speaker's lived experience of sickness causes her to think on the suffering of those who were burned alive in the nuclear attacks on Japan. Again, like with Plath's Holocaust poems, the use of a horrific historical event to highlight the speaker's personal pain is controversial for some readers. How could Plath, who did not experience the Holocaust, did not experience nuclear destruction, really understand what happened?

Popular Culture

One of the ways that confessional poetry influenced Plath was that it gave her permission to write about the mundane experience of everyday life—including popular or "low" culture. We can define *low culture* as items or experiences that have mass appeal—for example, consumer products like appliances or clothing, TV or movies, popular music, advertising, and celebrity gossip. Low culture exists in opposition to high culture, which refers to things like fine art, literature, opera, and ballet.

Plath was a savvy consumer of popular culture; after all, she had been a guest editor at *Mademoiselle*, a magazine that trafficked in fashion advice and contained copious advertising aimed young women. Plath's "process of *writing* fashion shows careful study and development; Plath was sensitive to descriptions of clothing in literature when developing her own, deeply evocative style," explains Plath critic Rebecca C. Tuite (Tuite, 2019, p. 134). *The Bell Jar* is filled with fashion moments, and Plath uses fashion to illustrate Esther's shifting psychological state. When Esther leaves New York City, for example, she throws her sophisticated internship wardrobe off the top of her building, instead favoring to wear a simple white blouse and folksy skirt—this shows that Esther is trying to access a part of herself that is purer and less artificial as she slides into depression.

As a writer and a person, Plath understood that fashion is a performance and a costume. In the poem "The Applicant," Plath writes about suits and their function as a costume of conformity and capitalism: "I notice you are stark naked./How about this suit—/Black and stuff, but not a bad fit," the speaker says. "It is waterproof, shatterproof, proof/Against fire and bombs through the roof./Believe me, they'll bury you in it."

Plath's poetry traffics in other popular cultural motifs as well. "Face Lift" is about plastic surgery, which, again, was not considered the stuff of poetry. "The Thin People" interrogates the medium of film and TV, questioning whether it has the power to help people remember traumatic events and potentially prevent them from happening. When Plath writes about the Rosenbergs' execution in her journal, she wonders if people would pay more attention if it were televised: "There is no yelling, no horror, no great rebellion. That is the appalling thing. The execution will take place tonight; it is too bad it cannot be televised . . . so much more realistic and beneficial than the run-of-the-mill crime program" (*Unabridged Journals* 2000, pp. 541–542). In "Lady Lazarus," Plath uses the act of striptease to examine the idea of spectacle; "the line 'What a million filaments' alludes to the electrical elements that produce a picture on a television or cinema scree, broadcasting the speaker's 'big striptease'" (Presley, 2019, p. 151).

Rebirth

Plath was fascinated by the idea of being reborn or resurrected. Her poetry and fiction are filled with references to rebirth. In *The Bell Jar*, Esther details her correctly administered electroshock therapy as something that wipes the slate clean, allows her to recover her mental health and reemerge from her traumatic experience as a new person. Plath's speakers and characters envy babies as pure creatures and take scalding hot baths to feel "pure and clean" again. In her poetry, Plath created a character called "Lady Lazarus" who performs a grotesque striptease of attempting suicide and being born again. Plath also writes of cosmetic surgery intended to give the person a completely new self, and she explores the liberation of the queen bee as a kind of rebirth. To say Plath was obsessed with concept of rebirth is an understatement.

The cycle of dying and coming back to life as something newer, better, more powerful is a part of ancient mythology from the Greeks to the Egyptians and many other cultures. Plath was interested in this mythology but also understood performative rebirth as a process that could benefit someone psychologically. For Plath, the ritual of being reborn fit in with her idea of suicide as a way of getting back to something that has been lost. The concept of rebirth is also often coupled with annihilation. The speaker or character often has to go through a harrowing experience that totally destroys her sense of self before she can be born again. Rebirth is a creative act that has destruction at its core— for in order to be reborn, one has to die first.

With every loss, Plath's poetic speakers attempt to redefine themselves and create something new from wreckage. Going through the process of rebirth unlocks creative powers. After all, writing a poem, and rewriting it, is a way to be reborn again and again.

The Sea

Many of the photographs we have of Plath show her at the beach, either sunbathing or in the water, and she considered the beach to be a healing place of great power. In a journal entry from 1951, Plath writes of the ocean's therapeutic powers after an experience at the beach rock climbing: "From this experience I emerge whole and clean, bitten to the bone by sun, washed pure by the icy sharpness of salt water, dried and bleached to the smooth tranquility that comes from dwelling among primal things (*Unabridged Journals*, 2000, pp. 75–76).

In Plath's poems, the sea is richly symbolic with multiple meanings. Depending on the poem, the sea is either a threat or a comfort; sometimes both at the same time. In *The Bell Jar*, Esther Greenwood attempts to drown herself, saying that it must be "the kindest way to die." However, Esther is unable to drown, as the ocean keeps spitting her back out, essentially trying to save her life. The ocean, which is classically associated with the feminine, is seen as a mother accepting and welcoming the child back into its womb; the sea can envelop the speaker in a warm embrace or potentially erase her.

Psychologically, the sea also represents the unconscious mind, a place as mysterious as the world beneath the waves. The sea is symbolic of self-annihilation in the face of something greater or more powerful. And on an ecological level, the sea represents the power of nature as well as nature's indifference to human existence; for Plath, the sea is sublime in the Romantic sense—something both terrifying and beautiful that reminds her of mortality.

Plath draws links "between the sea, her childhood, and her family. Her poems and prose breathe with longing and the melancholy of loss, as if she associates the loss of the sea with the loss of some mythological happy innocence" (Crowther, 2013, p. 225). Plath lived by the sea as a child and moved inland when her father died. In many of Plath's poems, such as "Full Fathom Five" and "The Colossus," the sea is associated with the loss of the father and represents the divide between them. In "Full Fathom Five," the father lives underneath the sea and occasionally pops up in a disturbing resurrection. In "The Colossus," Plath uses the image of the Colossus of Rhodes as a stand-in for a ruined father that needs to be put back together for the speaker to move on from her grief. One of the Seven Wonders of the Ancient World, the Colossus stood over the harbor on the island of Rhodes and was destroyed when an ancient earthquake snapped it at the knees, bringing it down.

In Plath's autobiographical essay, "Ocean 1212-W," she writes about her idyllic youth at the sea and how the loss of her childhood coincides with her father's death and moving inland. The loss of her father also becomes the loss of the sea, compounding Plath's grief.

The Self

Plath's ideas about the nature of the self permeate almost all of her writing. She was obsessed with the concept of self, especially the ways we mask our true selves. For Plath, the self is fragmentary or easily prone to fragmentation. Wholeness is a goal, but is often elusive. Plath's writing about the self includes references to costumes, performances, masks, suicide, and the act of writing itself, in which the self becomes mutable and myriad.

Plath's ideas about the self were influenced by psychoanalyst Sigmund Freud. At the time, Freudian ideas of the self were very popular in America and were a dominant ideology for explaining individual and relational psychology. Plath was "encouraged by her therapist, Dr. Ruth Beuscher, to explain herself to herself in Freudian terms and to fashion herself as a patient, an intellectual and artist by applying Freudian and other psychoanalytic doctrines and therapies" (Bundtzen, 2006, p. 37).

Id: Our instincts, untampered by social constraints. It is the source of desire, emotional impulse, bodily needs, and libido (sex drive).

Ego: The part of our personality where conscious awareness exists, the organized part of the personality, including intellectual-cognitive, executive, and perceptual functions. Our sense of self.

Superego: The internalization of cultural rules, taught by parents and other authority figures. Similar to a conscience, a drive that criticizes or prevents id-like behavior.

Plath's understanding of Freudian psychoanalysis, which is a psychological philosophy and practice developed and promoted by Sigmund Freud in the late 1800s and early 1900s, meant that Plath viewed herself and her mental health struggles through a Freudian lens. Freud was interested in the unconscious mind (organized by him as the id, ego, and superego) and how it fuels our behavior. He was also interested in how sexual repression could cause physical illness and the unconscious—often sexual—feelings children have for their parents (Freud coined the term "Oedipal Complex" after the Greek tragedy of Oedipus, who unknowingly killed his father and married his mother). Freud's theories have since been criticized as being misogynistic and sex-obsessed, but during the 1950s, Freud was popular.

Poems such as "Fever 103°" talk about "selves dissolving" as the speaker approaches a state of self-annihilation. "Lady Lazarus" expresses the removal of selves like a striptease or a mummy chuffing off its bandages to arrive at some essential core. Plath's thoughts about the self are complex and constantly evolved throughout her life. Sometimes, she appears to be saying that there is something fixed and essential about the self. Other times, she worries that there is no authentic self—just a series of imposed false selves that one must remove until there is nothing left. Whether or not that nothingness is frightening or liberating is debated.

Violence

Plath abhorred the conservative conventions of her day, and that disgust comes out most forcefully in her poetry. Many of Plath's poems contain violent imagery as well as narratives of violence: war, family conflict, destruction, animal relationships, abuse, and self-injury. Especially for a woman, it was considered inappropriate to write about these violent topics in such a graphic manner. Plath reveled in pushing buttons and exploring taboo issues, though, and her explorations of different kinds of violence paint a picture of a poet struggling to understand the human experience and the human capacity for cruelty—whether on a global scale, like genocide, or on an intimate scale, like domestic abuse.

Part of Plath's attraction to Ted Hughes's poetry was his unabashed use of extreme violence. In Hughes's poetry, animals kill, humans hurt each other in myriad ways, and the world appears indifferent to the ongoing violence of everyday life. Hughes also believed that we needed to be in touch with our animal selves, cultivate our animal instincts, and shed domesticity, and his poems demonstrate this desire. Plath shared Hughes's vision of humanity and how poems should play a role in exploring our repressed violent instincts.

In Hughes's life, he could be mean, as Sylvia notes in many letters to her mother: "Plath cautions her mother not to be shocked by a certain brutishness that Hughes cultivates. He stalks and bangs about, is a lady-killer, has a streak of cruelty in him—'cruel' is a word she uses several times to characterize him (Middlebrook, 2003, p. 36)." Plath was attracted to this cruelty, perhaps because it represented Hughes's rejection of the gentility she hated. In a 1962 interview with Peter Orr of the British Council, Plath discussed her impressions of English poetry of the time, noting that poetry needed to be tougher, bolder. English poetry, she said, was "in a bit of a strait-jacket, if I may say so. . . . I must say I am not very genteel and I feel that gentility has a stranglehold: the neatness, the wonderful tidiness, which is so evident everywhere in England is perhaps more dangerous than it would appear on the surface."

Writing

For Plath, writing is power and creation—and she often writes about writing in terms we can use to describe childbirth. When Plath writes about writing, she points to a medium that allows for the often uncomfortable slippage between the private and the public, the impersonal and the personal. Writing is power, and writing about the self is taking control of the narrative. In her poems about writing, Plath draws attention to the ways that women are allowed agency.

The poem "Ariel" is often interpreted as a writing journey. The poem begins with "stasis in darkness"—the moment before writing occurs. Then, as inspiration takes over the writer, she becomes "one" with the process, which is compared to riding a horse. The journey this writer takes as she becomes one with the writing (and riding) moves toward total annihilation as the writer actually ceases to be and becomes the poem. "I/am the arrow," Plath's speaker says, which references a phrase from *The Bell Jar* in which her boyfriend's mother tells her, "What a man is is an arrow into the future, and what a woman is is the place the arrow shoots off from."

In "Ariel," Plath speaks back to that moment and insists that she is the arrow; she has ambitions aside from being a housewife and is willing to push herself to the absolute limit to achieve her goals, even if it means self-destruction. Plath also writes about writing as spell work or doing magic—not in a "poof, here's a rabbit in a hat way," but in a primal, occult tradition with the writer as shaman or spirit medium. Hughes and Plath included some occult tools in their writing practice, such as a Ouija board and tarot cards—these objects are also referenced in some of Plath's poems.

THE POETRY

This section offers various interpretations of Plath's work—the context in which they were written, allusions, structure, word choice, and pertinent biographical information that might prove illuminating or simply just fun. I refer to other Plath scholars who have done excellent analytical work and research on Plath's poetry to offer a well-rounded view of how one poem contains ambiguity but is still an organized entity with stable thematic concerns. The selected poems are arranged chronologically so that you can trace the themes Plath uses and also see how her formal structures evolve over time.

"The Thin People" (1957)

Themes: The Holocaust, Violence

Plath wrote "The Thin People" in response to photographs and video footage she saw of the Holocaust. As journalists visited abandoned death camps and saw mass graves, starving human beings, and evidence of torture, they captured videos and took pictures. The horrors of the Holocaust then became visually real to the world. "The Thin People" asks: What do you do when confronted with images of evil? And what do those images mean for those who have been captured in them?

The poem is partly about the Holocaust but more about how we cannot forget these World War images that are now forever a part of our history. The poem refers to footage of Holocaust victims to discuss how we process images of traumatic events when we are not there to experience them firsthand. The poem also notes how the media makes the traumatic event permanent in images: "They are always with us, the thin people/Meager of dimension as the gray people/On a movie screen." The thin people are "forever drinking vinegar from tin cups," and "persevere in thinness," as if their suffering is occurring forever locked in those images and reproduced in film and books for eternity. Plath's speaker explores how time distances us from traumatic events, perhaps to our detriment.

Critic Tracy Brain suggests the poem "dramatises the tendency of photographic, journalistic, and cinematic representations to empty history of its three-dimensionality" (Brain, 2001, p. 37). Even as the speaker calls attention to the permanence of the image, she laments that our distance from the image prevents us from fully understanding traumatic events in history: ". . . we say:/ It was only in a movie, it was only/In a war making evil headlines . . . ." Essentially, Plath's work insists we must fight this distancing from historical events—in short, that we have a responsibility to remember.

"Full Fathom Five" (1958)

Themes: Rebirth, the Sea, the Self, Writing

"Full Fathom Five" is considered one of Plath's "father" poems. The death of Plath's father when she was eight was a formative and traumatic event in her life, and she returned to him again and again in her poetry. Plath's father, Otto, is usually treated as a larger-than-life figure who is menacing in some ways and pathetic in others. However, because we must always be careful to not conflate the speaker of the poem with the writer of the poem, Plath's "father" poems are not just about Otto Plath—they are poems about the universal idea of "the father." Plath's father poems also address other themes Plath frequently wrote about, such as grief, the sea, and rebirth.

In "Full Fathom Five," Plath mixes her thematic concerns to create a landscape that is both natural and mystical—an ocean that hides many secrets. Plath's poem introduces a god-like father figure who either appears to menace the speaker from a watery grave or magically comes back to life on occasion to remind the speaker of his presence. "Old man, you surface seldom./Then you come in with the tide's coming," Plath writes, referring to the old man's unpredictability. When will he turn up in her life? The speaker doesn't know.

The old man rises with white hair "miles long" and is covered in tangled rope. "Your dangers are many. I/Cannot look much," the speaker says, entranced but also repelled by the disturbing watery spectacle before her. Here, the ocean, like the father, is not a peaceful presence that brings the speaker comfort, but a primordial jungle of unknown things.

The title of the poem as well as other references throughout allude to William Shakespeare's play *The Tempest* (1611):

Full fathom five thy father lies;

Of his bones are coral made;

Those are pearls that were his eyes:

Nothing of him that doth fade

But doth suffer a sea-change

Into something rich and strange.

In this quote, the spirit Ariel addresses a young man who believes his father died in a shipwreck. The quote also reflects the ways in which the sea, and the island setting of *The Tempest*, has a strange and transformative power over people.

A major theme of *The Tempest* is the relationship between fathers and daughters. When a ship is wrecked on an island, the people on board are surprised to find Prospero, his daughter Miranda, and a magical spirit named Ariel already living on this island. Prospero is portrayed as a powerful man waiting to have his revenge on those who cast him and his daughter away on the island; he uses Ariel's magical powers to do his bidding. Prospero's daughter is a compassionate naïf who has only known life on the island—but she does not shirk from standing up to her father when she feels he is being unjust. She also ends up marrying for love.

Plath frequently references *The Tempest* in her poetry; it is a work that she seems to have related to as well as found literarily rich. Indeed, the title of *Ariel* also calls back to *The Tempest*; it refers to the spirit who is bound to work for the magician Prospero. Ariel wants to be set free, but he must perform all sorts of feats for Prospero before the magician will grant Ariel's wish (Ariel was also the name of a horse Plath sometimes rode).

"Full Fathom Five" is also a poem about fathers and daughters and the distance between them. The speaker cannot occupy the place where the father-sea god lives: "I walk dry on your kingdom's border/Exiled to no good" the speaker says, emphasizing that she occupies the space of the living and he the dead. But she wants to join him, explaining that she "would breathe water." The old man has a pull on the speaker and she may be in danger of joining him under the sea—because she misses the sea and what it represented to her as well as the loss of the father: "Father, this thick air is murderous./I would breathe water," the speaker says at the end of the poem. She is both frightened and in awe of the father figure, and she is grieving the loss of connection between them.

Critic Jo Gill has suggested that "Full Fathom Five" may be "understood as a play about deception and revelation, tyranny and enslavement—a drama in which family bonds are confused or betrayed and where the magical power of language is used to subjugate and silence as well as to create and heal" (Gill, 2006, p. 96). In this sense, Plath's use of references to *The Tempest* places her poetry in a larger literary context. She uses Shakespeare as a jumping-off point to explore the process of grieving, alienation, and the complexity of family relationships.

"Point Shirley" (1959)

Themes: Domesticity, the Sea

"Point Shirley" is poem that can be read as an elegy, or lament, for a dead place or a lost time that can never be regained. The tone is mournful as the speaker takes stock of an environment that used to be so alive with beautiful moments for her. The setting is a seaside home that has seen much joy as well as experienced the brutality of the sea. The poem also mourns a grandmother who was so expert at handling the rough storms that she cleaned up after sharks turned up in her geranium bed without batting an eyelash:

In my grandmother's sand yard. She is dead,

Whose laundry snapped and froze here, who

Kept house against

What the sluttish, rutted sea could do.

Plath spent her childhood living at the seaside in New England, and her earliest memories include time spent near or in the ocean. For Plath, the sea was a nurturing entity as well as one to be feared, for it could turn in an instant. As a young adult, nothing pleased Plath more than to take sun on the beach. In "Point Shirley" though, there is none of that. The town seems empty, with beach season over, and only the weathered residents battening down the hatches: she speaks of "The planked-up windows where she set/Her wheat loaves/And apple cakes to cool." The memory is so poignant, it's as if the speaker is shifting between two worlds. It's as if the speaker is walking through a ghost town. She sees the remnants of past times in the desolate landscape, like her grandmother's baking. The memories of happier times collide with the gray landscape she encounters in the present. "A labor of love, and that labor lost./Steadily the sea/Eats at Point Shirley," the speaker shares, remarking that no matter how we attempt to control and domesticate nature, it will eventually make everything its own.

Plath writes further about Point Shirley in her essay "Ocean 1212-W." Certain images, such as the shark in the garden, are repeated, but Plath adds more biographical elements to her essay, events such as the birth of her brother and death of her father, that colored her perspective on this seaside home.

In 1959, Plath was experimenting more by loosening her poetic structure, and "Point Shirley" seems to have pleased her as a development in her poetic practice. Plath wrote in her journals that she was particularly proud of "Point Shirley," explaining that it was "oddly powerful and moving to me in spite of a rigid formal structure. Evocative. Not so one dimensional" (*Unabridged Journals*, 2000, p. 463). Previous to "Point Shirley," Plath's work often adopted a formal structure. She wrote villanelles such as "Mad Girl's Love Song" as well as other poems that had strict rhyming patterns. She also felt that she repressed her language and fell too often into well-trod cliché (*Unabridged Journals,* 2000, p. 88.)

Plath would continue to experiment with structure and form, increasingly abandoning her self-perceived rigidity.

"The Colossus" (1959)

Themes: The Self, the Sea

Plath seemed to realize she was fixated on writing poems that included father figures; she wrote in her journal that "The Colossus" was a poem about "the old father-worship subject. But different. Weirder" *(Unabridged Journals,* 2000, p. 518). Considered an evolution of the themes in "Full Fathom Five," "The Colossus" shows Plath's shifting approach to a similar topic. Some of the differences include the tone and the choice of backstory. In "Full Fathom Five," Plath relied on *The Tempest* for her literary references and metaphors. In "The Colossus," she uses one of the Seven Wonders of the Ancient World, the Colossus of Rhodes.

In classical history, the Colossus of Rhodes was one of the Seven Wonders of the Ancient World. Located in the Greek isles, the Colossus stood approximately 108 feet high. It collapsed during an earthquake in 226 BCE, but parts of it have been preserved. Plath starts with a reference to this famous statue, one of the great architectural wonders—in ruins. It is the speaker's job to put it back together, but is the task completely futile? And what does the speaker get by taking on this monumental task?

In the first stanza, Plath sets an unusual scene. The speaker is "scaling little lasers with gluepot and pails of Lysol" in order to piece together an enormous, broken statue. Her initial assessment of the situation is pessimistic: "I shall never get you put together entirely," she says, and you can almost hear her sighing in resignation. This frustration is evident throughout the poem. The statue is speaking on "mule-bray, pig-grunt and bawdy cackles" so there is no shared language and communication isn't possible. This theme reoccurs in Plath's later poem "Daddy," where these grunts become the German language, and again, she is unable to comprehend: "I could never talk to you," the speaker says, noting that the German language is "obscene" and sticks in her jaw like a "barbed wire snare"—referencing Nazi death camps.

In a departure from "Full Fathom Five, the speaker is not as deferential to the father figure. It's a Sisyphian, or never-ending, task to her at this point: "Thirty years now I have labored/To dredge the silt from your throat./I am none the wiser." The silt in the throat blocks the Colossus from speaking, again suggesting that the speaker's task is futile and she will never receive the closure that comes with communication. But she has persisted for 30 years because completing this task could lead to her liberation. Through mourning the lost father figure, the speaker eventually finds her voice. However, the concluding stanza also suggests that the speaker is relegated to this task forever and will spend the rest of her life trying to put the past back together in a way that is meaningful and healing for her.

"Face Lift" (1961)

Themes: Domesticity, Mental Health, Rebirth, the Self

As an astute commenter on her cultural moment, Plath wrote poetry about traditional themes by using popular cultural touchstones—something that had been eschewed in poetry. Poetry was considered a "high art," meaning that poets were expected to be unconcerned with the stuff of every day and instead focus on lofty and universal topics. Plath had a talent for combining the high and the low, and "Face Lift" is a good example of how she uses cosmetic surgery to explore the philosophical idea of rebirth.

As a Cold War poet, Plath was sensitive to the oppressive beauty industry of the 1950s. She participated in traditionally feminine beauty rituals while lamenting the sexist philosophies behind them. Like many women of the time, Plath wore makeup, was interested in popular fashion, and was concerned with her appearance. She placed a great deal of import on appearances, connecting a healthy and attractive façade with a healthy emotional life. For Plath, these costumes of femininity were also costumes of mental health. As someone who had been hospitalized for a suicide attempt, she wanted to look as "normal" as possible during this paranoid historical moment when people were scrutinized for any unorthodox behavior or appearance.

In "Face Lift," Plath combines all of these concerns with the theme of rebirth. The speaker of the poem is a woman who has just had plastic surgery. Describing herself as wrapped in "mummy clothes," the speaker establishes that this is no ordinary facelift; there is much more at stake in this cosmetic procedure than smooth skin. The speaker compares herself to Cleopatra, which continues the reference to ancient Egyptians and their burial rituals, preparing the body of the dead for everlasting life in the afterworld. The speaker, "fizzy with sedatives" is made to "feel something precious" as "darkness wipes me out like chalk on a blackboard. . ." ("Face Lift"). This same line—"darkness wiped me out like chalk on a blackboard" is also used in *The Bell Jar* during the scene when Esther is receiving her first positive experience with electroconvulsive therapy. It's not coincidental that Plath associates electroconvulsive therapy with cosmetic surgery. Electroconvulsive therapy, when done correctly, provides Esther with the sense that she has gone backward in time to a moment when health and newness were possible.

After five days of recovery, the poetic speaker describes what she has really been looking for: not smoother skin but a brand-new self. "They've traded her in some laboratory jar./Let her die there," the speaker says of her old face/old self. She has been reborn: "Mother to myself, I wake swaddled in gauze./Pink and smooth as a baby." The speaker, assisted by the surgeon, has completed the process of rebirth and is now a totally different person, freed from the desiccated trappings of her former self. She has been reborn, thanks to modern science. But, can it really be that simple, Plath seems to ask us. Has the speaker really been able to transcend her troubles? The poem leaves us with an ambiguous conclusion.

"Morning Song" (1961)

Themes: Motherhood, the Self, Writing

Biographically, "Morning Song" was written about Plath's daughter, Frieda's birth. But as with all of Plath's poems, this biographical tidbit does not tell the entire story. A poem that explores the joy and fear that accompanies becoming a mother, "Morning Song" is both tender and anxious, reveling in new birth but also expressing fear.

The poem's opening lines, "Love set you going like a fat gold watch./The midwife slapped your footsoles, and your bald cry/Took its place among the elements" introduce the connection between birth and language. As the opening poem in Plath's version of *Ariel*, love, writing, and birth set the tone for the collection; thus, "Morning Song" is not only about the birth of a child but the birth of a book. Placing this poem first in the collection is significant because it "commemorates both Frieda's and *Ariel's* genesis as an act of love"

(Bundtzen, 2001, p. 129). This poem might be about the birth of a baby, but it is also about the rebirth of a writer learning to master a new language: the groundbreaking language of the *Ariel* poems.

The speaker of "Morning Song" is a woman who acts on instinct, who is domestic, and who is unsure. She is an almost humorous character "cow-heavy and floral/In my Victorian nightgown" as she hurries out of bed to check on the baby in the crib and make sure she is still breathing. It's something that all new parents do, obsessively stare for that rising of the chest, listen for that exhalation and inhalation. "I wake to listen:/A far sea moves in my ear," the speaker says, further reinforcing the maternal connection to the ocean.

The poem also expresses the range of emotions new parents experience. Critic Diane Middlebrook suggests that "Morning Song" is "about a woman's gradual acquisition of an emotional bond with her newborn" (Middlebrook, 2006, p. 161). Middlebrook traces the trajectory of the poem from "dread" to "connection." With the vowels rising in the last stanza, "the infant has ascended from mere animate existence into human being she can recognize—whom she can love. Now she becomes a mother" (Middlebrook, 2006, p. 162). And, I would suggest, a fully realized writer.

"Tulips" (1961)

Themes: Flowers, Mental Health, Rebirth, the Self

Plath wrote "Tulips" in the aftermath of a miscarriage and appendicitis. In a journal entry from February 27, 1961, Plath explains that she is about to have surgery to remove the appendix, and we get a vision of the flowers in Plath's hospital room—the flowers that will become the subject of "Tulips": "All night they've been breathing in the hall dropping their pollens, daffodils, pink & red tulips, the hot purple & red eyed—anemones." In this journal entry, we already see the flowers being personified as threatening entities; about a month later on March 18, Plath would complete "Tulips," where the flowers are referred to as "dangerous animals."

On the surface, "Tulips" is a poem about recovering from surgery, but when you examine how Plath treats the flowers, it becomes clear that the poem is about death—or, more specifically, the seductive power of death. The speaker is recovering in the hospital "learning peacefulness" and slowly losing her identity: "I am nobody." The speaker enjoys being treated like a patient, being positioned in the bed and fussed over while she is brought "numbness in their bright needles." As she falls further into medicated stupor, she relishes the nothingness: "Now I have lost myself I am sick of baggage," she says as reminders of life such as the smiles from a family photograph "catch onto my skin, little smiling hooks." She wants to forget her life so she can cease to exist—but she is surrounded by reminders of her family that refuse to let her slip into oblivion.

Like Plath's poems about rebirth, "Tulips" tells the story of a woman who wants to transition to another state of being, to cross over to a place where she doesn't have to be bothered with earthly concerns. She imagines this state of being as something close to death:

I didn't want any flowers, I only wanted

To lie with my hands turned up and be utterly empty.

How free it is, you have no idea how free —

The peacefulness is so big it dazes you,

And it asks nothing, a name tag, a few trinkets.

It is what the dead close on, finally;

The tulips in the speaker's hospital room are violent reminders of life that she cannot fade away. "'Tulips' contrasts the seductively anesthetic blankness of the hospital setting with the 'sudden tongues' of the red flowers which 'hurt' the speaker back into life, and implicitly writing," suggests critic Christina Britzolakis (2006, p. 112). The tulips are "excitable," they "hurt" her with their too-red-ness, they watch her and make loud noises that break the speaker out of her drugged reverie: "They concentrate my attention, that was happy/Playing and resting without committing itself." They drag her away from her death wish with their color and ground her back in the physical world. "I have wanted to efface myself," the speaker says, but the tulips prevent her from doing so. The hospital setting, always a fraught space for Plath, presents a contrast between death and life, giving up and fighting, destroying and creating.

"Elm" (1962)

Themes: Domesticity, Motherhood, the Self, Writing

"Elm" is a poem that many critics believe was a major turning point in Sylvia Plath's work. Tracy Brain looks at the labor involved in bringing the poem to its final state, noting that Plath wrote thirteen drafts and two typescripts of "Elm"

(Brain, 2001, p. 105). Plath gives the elm tree a voice and genders it as female. The speaker and the subject of the poem cross boundaries in an uncomfortable way, and Plath purposefully makes the reader question who, or what, is the agent in this poem. She even had to explain the poem to her editor at *The New Yorker*, who had questions about the poem's point of view: "The 'she says' is the elm. The whole poem is the elm talking & might be in quotes. The elm is talking to the woman who contemplates her—they are intimately related in mood, and the various moods, I think, of anguish, are explored . . ." (*Letters Vol. 2*, 2018, p. 815). A few months later, Plath is elated to discover that her poem will be published in *The New Yorker*: "I am happier to have you take this than about any of the other poems you have taken—I thought it might be a bit too wild and bloody, but I'm glad it's not" (*Letters Vol. 2*, 2018, p. 853).

At this point in her career, Plath was becoming more interested in mythology and occult symbolism, and the language these disciplines gave her fueled the "wild and bloody" poems of this time. The symbolism of the elm tree is especially significant, as it is associated with rebirth. For Plath, the ritual of dying must occur in order for the fullest version of the self to be triumphantly reborn.

The elm itself is wise and old and has seen humankind triumph and fail. The elm knows truth, deeply: "I know the bottom, she says. I know it with my great tap root:/It is what you fear./I do not fear it: I have been there." The elm's story is one of being brutalized by the elements, by "the atrocity of sunsets," the "merciless" moon, "wind of such violence." "I am terrified by this dark thing/ That sleeps in me;" the elm says, perhaps giving voice to the speaker's fear as the two commune.

At the end of the poem, it seems as if the elm tree and the woman reach a point of radical merging: "What is this, this face/So murderous in its strangle of branches?—" The woman comes face to face with herself in the form of the tree. They share a commonality; both have been used and are forced to withstand hardship. Like the gorgon Medusa, who is invoked with her "snaky acids," the speaker and the tree are cast as pariahs.

The merging of woman and nature represents a shift in Plath's conception of her own femininity as well as ecological concerns in the context of nuclear fallout. Women and nature have always been linked in popular consciousness, epitomized in the figure of Mother Nature. And remember all those stories about witches heading into the forest to dance around naked, or whatever people thought women temporarily escaping the confines of domesticity did.

"The Applicant" (1962)

Themes: Domesticity, Popular Culture

This is one of Plath's most overtly critical poems of Cold War culture. It even uses the language of Cold War consumerism and advertising to cast an unflattering light on conformity culture, especially including marriages that seem more like job interviews and intimate relationships treated like business transactions. The poem begins with the jarring line "First, are you our sort of person?" According to Tracy Brain's reading of the poem, "the question is a challenge or warning that equally haunts men and women...'sort of person' is a euphemism for a marriage, heterosexual, middle-class, anti-Communist consumer (Brain, 2001, p. 200).

In "The Applicant," women don't fare any better than men. Women are referred to as "it" instead of "she," which reinforces their objectification: "A living doll, everywhere you look./It can sew, it can cook,/It can talk, talk, talk." The women being peddled to this applicant are like robots, only necessary for the domestic labor and banal conversation they provide: "The Applicant" interprets the ideological emphasis on marriage and family as a scare tactic disguised as the promise of fulfillment. It's a bleak portrait of domestic arrangements in the 1950s and an argument for how human relationships are essentially transforming into professional exchanges devoid of the messiness of humanity.

The speaker, a kind of slick salesperson, appears to be talking to a man, someone who may have sustained injuries during the war. The speaker is telling this applicant—it appears he is applying for a bride—that he needs to find the right suit (after all, the suit makes the man).

Black and stiff, but not a bad fit.

Will you marry it?

It is waterproof, shatterproof, proof

Against fire and bombs through the roof.

Believe me, they'll bury you in it.

In Sloan Wilson's popular 1955 novel, *The Man in the Gray Suit*, protagonist Tom Rath and his family struggle to find meaning in a world increasingly anonymous and corporatized world. Struggling with PTSD from his war service,

Tom has to make a choice to essentially kill himself working or abandon his dreams of a middle-class suburban existence to restore happiness to his life. "The Applicant" is reminiscent of this contemporaneous novel, as the suit—symbolic of the repression and conformity of 1950s culture—is essentially a kind of prison suit that's supposed to protect you from the horrors of the day. But in exchange for safety and protection, you will have to die in that suit, as anonymously as you were while wearing it. The black suit, Plath implies, will not save you.

"The Rabbit Catcher" (1962)

Themes: Domesticity, Violence

"The Rabbit Catcher" was one of the poems that Ted Hughes chose to excise from the published version of *Ariel*, which perhaps tells us that he saw himself in Plath's exploration of a violent relationship and wanted to save face. "The Rabbit Catcher" is a singular poem in that it has generated a great deal of criticism, both focusing on the work itself and how it has been censored in the past.

The reader is immediately thrown into a hostile environment and then bombarded with images of violence for the duration of the poem: "It was a place of force—/The wind gagging my mouth with my own blown hair,/Tearing off my voice," the poem begins. The speaker is placed in a setting in which the weather is dangerous and renders her speechless; as we see in other Plath poems, being deprived of the ability to speak puts the speaker in a perilous, disempowered position. The words "gagging" and "tearing" also have an element of sexual violence as well. Even the flowers (the gorse) in the landscape are portrayed as violent, "malignant" entities. They are described as having "black spikes" and being "extravagant, like torture."

Though the speaker is introduced as a human, she also identifies with and perhaps even becomes the rabbit of the title, being chased into its rabbit hole, trying to escape the hunter and the snares he has set out. Then she introduces the metaphor of the tea mug, a delicate item being manhandled: "I felt hands round a tea mug, dull, blunt,/Ringing the white china./How they awaited him, those little deaths!/They waited like sweethearts. They excited him." Here, the speaker becomes the tea mug as it is being choked, introducing the possibility of a domestic violence scenario. The poem concludes with the speaker mourning the loss of her agency as well as a relationship:

And we, too, had a relationship—

Tight wires between us,

Pegs too deep to uproot, and a mind like a ring

Sliding shut on some quick thing,

The constriction killing me also.

Biographer Diane Middlebrook suggests that "The Rabbit Catcher" can be read as a short story: "A woman is walking on a hot day in the countryside when she spots a line of snares set by a rabbit catcher. She imagines the man who set them as waiting in his own kitchen in a state akin to sexual arousal, and envisions her husband as this man, and herself as his prey" (Middlebrook, 2003, p. 169). The hunter/husband is the predator and the rabbit/speaker is his hunt, a defenseless animal whose best strategy is to hide in a hole, effectively minimizing herself.

Critics have noted the similarities between "The Rabbit Catcher" and two of D.H. Lawrence's poems, "Love on the Farm" and "Rabbit Snared in the Night." D.H. Lawrence, who was one of Plath's favorite writers, influenced her thoughts on human nature and humanity's capacity for violent, animal acts.

"Stings" (1962)

Themes: Bees and Beekeeping, Domesticity, Rebirth, the Self, Violence, Writing

In October 1962, Plath wrote a remarkable series of poems known as the "bee cycle." I discuss this cycle in more depth in Chapter 6, as all of these bee poems should be studied as a unit in order to get the fullest sense of Plath's goal. The five poems included are "The Bee Meeting," "The Arrival of the Bee Box," "Stings," "The Swarm," and "Wintering." However, "Stings" is often studied on its own because it provides a vital look at Plath's feelings toward domesticity and creativity and how they can be incompatible in the best situation, untenable in the worst.

Having written about the perils of 1950s domesticity and how it saps women of their creative spirit and renders them solely dull husband-helpers and mothers, in the bee cycle, Plath transforms her cultural criticism into the story of the queen bee and the female beekeeper. Loosely, the trajectory of the cycle moves from the speaker's insecurity and feelings of alienation about beekeeping and the beekeeping community to identification with the queen bee and finally with a hopeful gaze toward a world absent of patriarchal dictates ("They have got rid of the men," the speaker announces in "Wintering").

In "Stings" specifically, Plath writes about the plight of the aging queen bee who the speaker imagines has been abused. But the speaker thinks of and tends to the aging queen with tenderness and empathy. In a shift from the earlier poems in the bee cycle, the speaker is now confident with her ability to handle bees. She is "bare-handed" as she hands the combs to another beekeeper, combs taken from her hive that she has decorated with pink flowers and "excessive love." She imagines the queen bee is old, "her wings torn shawls, her long body/Rubbed of its plush—/Poor and bare and unqueenly and even shameful." The queen has seen better days, the speaker intimates. The speaker has also seen better days, too: "I am no drudge/Though for years I have eaten dust/And dried plates with my dense hair./And seen my strangeness evaporate." The speaker aligns herself with the queen, explaining how domesticity has stolen her beauty and her sense of self.

The speaker is further aligned with the bees when she refers to a third person (possibly the speaker's husband) in the poem who is watching the speaker interact with the other beekeeper. He is unprepared to handle the bees, wearing only linen. The bees attack him, possibly to the speaker's delight, "molding onto his lips like lies,/Complicating his features." After the third person runs away from the bees, the speaker appears triumphant. She controls the bees, she implies. And with this third person gone, she can rise and reclaim her title of queen:

> They thought death was worth it, but I
>
> Have a self to recover, a queen.
>
> Is she dead, is she sleeping?
>
> Where has she been,
>
> With her lion-red body, her wings of glass?
>
> Now she is flying
>
> More terrible than she ever was, red
>
> Scar in the sky, red comet
>
> Over the engine that killed her—
>
> The mausoleum, the wax house.

In these lines, the speaker reasserts her value in a world that sees her as a second-class citizen. She is empowered by the flight of the queen bee, who is viewed as liberating herself from the hive. However, once the elder queen bee leaves the hive, she is likely to be replaced by a newer, younger queen. Still, in "Stings," this risk seems worth it. Written after discovering her husband's infidelity, perhaps Plath was using the bee cycle as a way to work through her husband leaving her for another woman.

"Fever 103°" (1962)

Themes: Flowers, Nuclear War, Rebirth, the Self

Plath feared nuclear warfare from a very early age. Growing up in the wake of the American bombings of Hiroshima and Nagasaki in 1945, Plath was horrified by descriptions of atomic bombing victims and the devastation of the attack. In her journals and letters, Plath criticized what she perceived as the American craze for nuclear domination and lamented the destruction of life. Plath's pacifism extended into her adult life, as she later attended a "Ban the Bomb" event while living in England.

Nuclear war is a dominant theme in "Fever 103°," a poem that explores female sexuality as well as illness. Plath wrote the poem on October 20, 1962, one day after penning a letter to her friend Clarissa Roche about being sick with a fever, the impending divorce with Hughes, and her need for company. When Plath read the poem on the BBC, she introduced it as a poem about "two kinds of fire—the fires of hell, which merely agonize, and the fires of heaven, which purify."

The poem uses a diverse array of images and references Greek mythology, nuclear war, flowers, Hiroshima, Christianity (in particular Catholicism), female sexuality, and a famous, dead modern dancer named Isadora Duncan. All of these references work together with short lines and hyphenation to create a frenetic tapestry that is the mind of a feverish woman. The poem starts with a rhetorical question that haunts the speaker and reader throughout: "Pure? What does it mean?"

When the speaker asks what purity means, it sets up the poem to answer that question. But purity can refer to purity of spirit, purity of body, purity of mind, and purity of art. In "Fever 103°," all of these different kinds of purity are addressed. Plath wrote feverishly during this time and associated that creative force with transformative power. However, as she mentioned in the BBC interview, there is always a light and dark side, and this feverish, creative force could also be potentially destructive; that's what Plath is trying to convey in the poem.

The speaker of "Fever 103°" begins her journey toward self-transformation in a hellscape of fire and monsters—in particular Cerberus, who in Greek mythology is a massive, three-headed dog that guards Hades, the Underworld. The speaker, then, is either attempting to escape Hades or preparing to enter. She invokes "Isadora's scarves," referring to the famous modern dancer Isadora Duncan who died when her scarf got caught in the wheel of an automobile and broke her neck. Duncan was a woman who flaunted convention and lived a flamboyant and eventually destructive life; she was the positive and negative of the creative spirit embodied.

Plath's speaker references flowers, in particular a hothouse "ghastly orchid." The hothouse orchid is a very delicate plant raised in a special environment—it's probably unlikely to be able to survive a transition to the outside environment. The orchid is associated with the feminine, and this particular orchid symbolizes the female domestic, trapped and stifled in the home and unable to survive on its own. "Hothouse flower" typically is used as a metaphor for a person who is fragile and sheltered, and a hothouse flower must be cared for with great attention. Similarly, an animal that is rendered unable to survive on its own in the poem is the leopard, who is killed by nuclear radiation. The fires of hell produce "Hiroshima" ash, which highlights the geopolitical reality of living during the age of nuclear war and the absolute power of the nuclear bomb to annihilate all living things.

The speaker rapidly moves from this hallucinatory hellscape to the hell of her own bed, where she lies in fever unable to sleep or eat: "Three days. Three nights./Lemon water, chicken/Water, water make me retch." The three days and three nights is a reference to Jesus rising from the dead on the third day, emphasizing the poem's theme of self-transformation and rebirth. "Reminiscent in cadence, image and harmfulness of that all-pervasive water in Coleridge's 'The Rime of the Ancient Mariner,' this water is both treatment for and cause of her illness," notes Tracy Brain, drawing connections between "Fever 103°" and Samuel Taylor Coleridge's classic poem. In "The Rime of the Ancient Mariner," a mariner scoffs at fate by killing an albatross, which then causes his ship to encounter all kinds of calamity, including the death of the crew one by one. The famous (and often misquoted line) "Water, water, every where,/ Nor any drop to drink" refers to the sea, which if consumed leads to dehydration and madness.

The speaker of the poem eventually attains a state that seems like transformative annihilation. She becomes pure from the harrowing experience, saying that she is a "Virgin/attended by roses," "(My selves dissolving, old whore petticoats)—/To Paradise." In equivocating herself with the Virgin Mary, the speaker becomes beatific, untouchable, transcendent. She has gone through the fire and become cleansed.

"Daddy" (1962)

Themes: The Holocaust, Mental Health, Rebirth, the Self, Violence, Writing

Perhaps Plath's most famous poem, "Daddy," is, on the surface, about fathers. But it's about so much more. Following the trajectory of "Full Fathom Five" and "The Colossus," "Daddy" departs from those two "father" poems in radical formal and thematic ways. We still have the image of the larger-than-life father—the daughter-speaker in the poem says she has been living in his black shoe like a foot—but now the father has become a literal Nazi, the ultimate symbol of evil and oppression.

The use of repetition and the rhythm of "Daddy" lends to its feeling of ominousness. The poem is relentless, churning, chant-like. It borrows from the structure of fairy-tale rhymes, but the violent content provides a disturbing juxtaposition. The first two lines, "You do not do, you do not do/Any more, black shoe," exemplify the emphasis on assonance—the repetition of a vowel sound. Critic Steven Gould Axelrod notes, "The first line seems less than articulation than a presymbolic scream" (Axelrod, 2006, p. 82). The "oo" sound continues throughout the poem, creating an auditory pattern that is "propulsive, compulsive, redundant, wild" (p. 82). Axelrod also explains that while the poem starts in the language of a child, it quickly "adopts a distinctly adult vocabulary . . . this collision of discourse types reflects the poem's journey back in time to uncover a repression and reexperience a deidealized past" (p. 83). There is something childlike in the speaker's yearning and anger for the lost father she mourns—but that this childlike rage exists within an adult speaker creates a disturbing tone.

"Daddy" grapples with not just fathers but husbands and patriarchal oppression. The poem shifts from addressing the father to addressing the husband: "I made a model of you, A man in black with a Meinkampf look/And a love of the rack and the screw./And I said I do, I do." Here, we see the repetition of the "you do not do" with the "I do"—the marriage vow—which connects the father to the husband. The speaker did not have a choice in her father's death, but she did have a choice to marry a man that reminded her of him. Both are characterized by Nazi imagery: the husband's "Meinkampf look" and the father's "Luftwaffe, your gobbledygoo./And your neat mustache/And your Aryan eye, bright blue." The line "Every woman adores a fascist" has been discussed at length, with many critics seeing the reference as tongue-in-cheek—a dark joke about how women are magically predestined to flock to cruel men, thus making their abuse their own fault. In reality, the speaker fights to escape the abuse she's experienced at the hands of the father and the husband. Is she successful? The last line of the poem, "Daddy, daddy, you bastard, I'm through," can be read as a triumph or a defeat.

This is how Plath described the poem for the BBC: "Here is a poem spoken by a girl with an Electra Complex. Her father died while she thought he was God. Her case is complicated by the fact that her father was also a Nazi and her mother very possibly part Jewish. In the daughter the two strains marry and paralyze each other—she has to act out the awful little allegory once over before she is free of it."

According to psychoanalyst Carl Jung, the *Electra Complex* is a girl's psychosexual competition with her mother for possession of her father. This theory is similar to Sigmund Freud's conceptualization of the Oedipal Complex, which refers to a boy's psychosexual competition with his father for possession of his mother.

"Daddy" was a revolutionary poem for its time and inspired poets to address more taboo subjects in radical ways. Indeed, it changed the landscape for poetry, encouraging future poets to grapple with difficult, taboo material.

"Lady Lazarus" (1962)

Themes: Domesticity, the Holocaust, the Self, Violence, Writing, Rebirth

For many, "Lady Lazarus" is the poem that most conveys the standard Sylvia Plath mythology—a first-person glimpse into the mind of an angry, suicidal woman who eats men "like air." But there's so much more going on. The poem can be seen as a complex response to having one's trauma objectified and com-moditized. It asks questions of power and agency, and paints a bleak portrait of a world in which survivors of violence are asked to put themselves on display. It is a desperate search for selfhood in a world that doesn't value life.

"Lady Lazarus" brings together many of the themes Plath writes about in other poems: the self, mental illness, consumerism, the Holocaust, and creating art. The tone is glib, sarcastic, bitter, and menacing, and Plath mixes imagery from the Holocaust, Samuel Taylor Coleridge's poem "Kubla Khan," the world of sex work, and the Bible.

The story of Lazarus comes from the New Testament of the Bible. Lazarus, whom Jesus loves, is ill. Lazarus' sisters ask Jesus to come quickly to help their brother, but Jesus delays two days. When he finally arrives, he finds that Lazarus has died. Lazarus' sisters are angry that Jesus did not come in time. Jesus tells them to take him to Lazarus' tomb. There, he rolls the rock from the entrance, prays, and tells Lazarus to come out. In a miraculous event, Lazarus rises from the dead and leaves the tomb wearing his shroud.

Plath was interested in the story of Lazarus, perhaps because she felt the story spoke to her as a survivor of a suicide attempt. She wrote in her journal on June 15, 1959, that she had an idea for a short story: "MENTAL HOSPITAL STORIES: Lazarus theme. Come back from the dead. Kicking off thermometers. Violent ward. LAZARUS MY LOVE" (*Unabridged Journals,* 2000, p. 497). "Lazarus My Love" was never completed, but the reference to this spectacular mythical person turned up in *Ariel* three years later. Clearly, Lazarus had significant cultural meaning for Plath.

"Lady Lazarus" can be seen as a modern retelling of the story of Lazarus, but with a few twists. First, Lady Lazarus speaks. In this first-person poem, she tells us what she wants us to know about her experience; she gives a silenced woman a voice. Second, Lady Lazarus has died three times and come back each time:

I am only thirty.

And like a cat I have nine times to die.

This is Number Three.

What a trash

To annihilate each decade.

Thirdly, there is no sanctity for the tomb and the "ritual" of rising from the dead/being reborn. The setting is like a circus, with the speaker cast as a circus freak: "The peanut-crunching crowd/shoves in to see/Them unwrap me hand and foot—/The big strip tease." This is a spectacle, and the speaker is an exhibitionist offering her body up for the crowd to gawk at: "For the eyeing of my scars, there is a charge," she says almost smugly.

During the era of McCarthyism, with its emphasis on surveillance, Lady Lazarus is a figure in control of what she reveals and what she conceals (Nelson, 2002, p. 33). In this way, she can be seen as playing with the cultural demand to tell secrets—to confess. Through the speaker, Plath asks: How much power do women have over their own bodies and stories? Does turning your body into a commodity, like Lady Lazarus does by charging them to see her, give you power? "Lady Lazarus, under the protection of her own death, can say anything," argues Lisa Narbeshuber. "She has nothing left to lose. . .she occupies a position of strength, power, and privilege" (Narbeshuber, 2004, p. 196). She is also an artist—and a very accomplished one at that: "Dying/Is an art, like everything else. I do it exceptionally well."

Plath uses references to the Holocaust such as a "Nazi lampshade," "a cake of soap," "ash," and "a gold filling." She also uses the German language when speaking to males in positions of power: "Herr Doktor," "Herr God," and "Herr Lucifer." What to make of a poem that relies so heavily on symbols of the Holocaust? In 1951, philosopher Theodor Adorno famously said, "No poetry after Auschwitz," meaning that after the atrocities of the Holocaust, language was rendered inadequate. Here, Plath seems to insist that there must be poetry after Auschwitz, that without poetry there is forgetting—similar to the message in "The Thin People."

Poetry Terms Defined (from *The Bedford Glossary of Critical and Literary Terms*)

Alliteration: The repetition of sounds in a sequence of words. Alliteration generally refers to repeated consonant sounds (often initial consonant sounds).

Allusion: An indirect reference to a person, event, statement, or theme found in literature, the other arts, history, mythology, religion, or popular culture.

Ambiguity: The result of something being stated in such a way that its meaning cannot be definitely determined.

Assonance: The repetition of identical or similar vowel sounds, usually in stressed syllables, followed by different consonant sounds in proximate words.

Elegy: Typically used to refer to reflective poems that lament the loss of something or someone (or loss or death more generally).

Enjambment: A poetic expression that spans more than one line. Lines exhibiting enjambment do not end with grammatical breaks, and their sense is not complete without the following line(s).

Form: Either the general type or the unique structure of a literary work. Form can also be used generally to refer to rhyme patterns, metrical arrangements, and so forth. . . . The term is often used more specifically, however, to refer to the singular structure of a particular work.

Free Verse: Poetry that lacks a regular meter, does not rhyme, and uses irregular (and sometimes very short) line lengths. Writers of free verse disregard traditional poetic conventions of rhyme and meter, relying instead on parallelism, repetition, and the ordinary cadences and stresses of everyday discourse.

Hyperbole: A figure of speech that uses deliberate exaggeration to achieve an effect, whether serious, comic, or ironic.

Imagery: A term used to refer to (1) the actual language that a writer uses to convey a visual picture for; and (2) the use of figures of speech, often to express abstract ideas in a vivid and innovative way. Imagery of this second type makes use of such devices as simile, personification, and metonymy, among many others.

Irony: A contradiction or incongruity between appearance or expectation and reality.

Lyric: Today, a brief melodic and imaginative poem (as opposed to a narrated tale) characterized by the fervent structured expression of private thoughts and emotions by a single speaker who speaks in the first person.

Metaphor: A figure of speech that associates two unlike things; the representation of one thing by another.

Meter: The more or less regular pattern of accented and unaccented syllables in poetry.

Personification: A figure of speech that bestows human characteristics on anything nonhuman, from an abstract idea to a physical force to an inanimate object to a living organism.

Rhyme: Generally, the repetition of identical vowel sounds in the stressed syllables of two or more words as well as of all subsequent sounds after this vowel sound.

Rhythm: A term referring to a measured flow of words and signifying the basic (though often varied) beat or pattern in language that is established by stressed syllables, unaccented syllables, and pauses.

Simile: A figure of speech that compares two essentially unlike things by using words such as *like* or *as* to link the vehicle and the tenor.

Tone: The attitude of the author toward the reader or the subject matter of a literary work.

Chapter 4
The Bell Jar,
Short Fiction,
and Essays

INTRODUCTION TO THE FICTION

"I think I'll be a pretty good novelist," Plath wrote to her brother Warren in 1963. "My stuff makes me laugh & laugh, & if I can laugh now it must be hellishly funny stuff." Based on *The Bell Jar*, Plath probably would have been a good novelist. Unfortunately, *The Bell Jar* remains Plath's only published novel. We know, based on journal entries and letters, that Plath was working on at least two other novels. *Falcon Yard* was based on Plath's experiences as a student in Cambridge and followed the trajectory of a young woman trying to find herself abroad through romantic relationships and travel. According to Plath's mother, Plath burned the manuscript of *Falcon Yard* in the courtyard of her Devon home after Plath intercepted a phone call from Ted Hughes's mistress, Assia Wevill (Ferreter, 2011, p. 13).

Double Exposure or *Doubletake* was to be Plath's third and last novel, on which she started working in 1962. She told her benefactor, Olive Higgins Prouty, that the story was about a woman who had adored her husband but he then leaves her for another woman. The manuscript for this novel is missing. Some allege that Hughes may have destroyed it, as he admitted to destroying one of Plath's journals that detailed the last several months of her life "because I did not want her children to read it." In the Introduction to *Johnny Panic and the Bible of Dreams*, Hughes claims that *Double Exposure* "disappeared somewhere around 1970" (p. 1).

Although *The Bell Jar* remains the only full example we have of Plath's long fiction writing, there are numerous short stories and essays demonstrating Plath's interest in experimenting with plot, characterization, and symbolism. Like her poetry, Plath's fiction shows her keen interest in criticizing Cold War culture, sexual double standards, and gender inequality. Her fiction also focuses on death, mental health, and parenting. As a fiction writer, Plath creates a strong sense of place in all her pieces that guides the reader toward understanding her perspective. Whether it is the sea, a medical office, a forest, or a freezing cold apartment, Plath's settings are almost characters in their own right, vivid and imbued with emotional complexity and precise detail.

THE BELL JAR

The Bell Jar is a mental health coming-of-age story (*bildunsgroman*) about a young woman trying to find herself in an environment she considers hostile. But it is also a story about the Cold War, gender politics, conformity culture, and authenticity. In this way, it is a mirror of America in Plath's own time. Plath indicts conformity culture for leading to protagonist Esther Greenwood's mental collapse. Esther cannot have it all, Plath seems to be saying, and trying to navigate this world where she is discouraged from writing, exploring her sexuality, and embarking on a less-conventional life causes Esther to attempt suicide. Esther must learn to heal from a traumatic summer and discover her worth as a woman and a writer through hospitalization, therapy, and sexual liberation. She needs to shed the false selves that are keeping her sick and embrace life on her own terms. Many of the novel's major themes overlap with those of Plath's poetry.

The Bell Jar is fiction, but it was loosely based on Plath's own experiences as an intern at *Mademoiselle* magazine and the months after, including her struggle with depression, suicide attempt, and recovery at a psychiatric hospital. Written in the first person, it's easy to conflate Esther with Plath. Esther and Plath share many similarities. They are both women with writing ambitions. Both of their fathers are dead. They are both competitive and intelligent. Esther's suicide attempt mirrors Sylvia's. And both women find a mother-figure in a brilliant and modern-minded female psychiatrist. However, it's crucial for readers to remember that Esther is a creation, the result of Plath's using the tools of fiction to make larger statements about female experience during the 1950s.

Plath did not write about this time in her life very much in her journals; there's a gap, which is uncharacteristic since Plath's journal writing was prolific. From May 14 to July 1953, there are only a few fragments: "New York, pain, parties, work. And Gary and ptomaine—and Jose the cruel Peruvian and Carol vomiting outside the door all over the floor — and interviews for TV shows, & competition, and beautiful models and Miss Abels . . . And now this: shock. Utter nihilistic shock" *(Unabridged Journals*, 2000, p. 187), and her outrage over the Rosenbergs' execution as previously noted. However, scholars have theorized based on letters, witness accounts, calendar entries, and other writings that Plath mined her own experiences extensively to create the world of *The Bell Jar*.

The Bell Jar is a first-person narrative told in the past tense. It begins with Esther Greenwood living in New York City and experiencing symptoms of depression. We soon learn, in a very throwaway moment that you might almost miss, that Esther is relaying her story from the present. She refers to souvenirs from her time in New York: "for a long time afterward I hid them away, but later, when I was all right again, I brought them out, and I still have them around the house . . . last week I cut the plastic starfish off the sunglasses case for the baby to play with." This moment is brief but important; it establishes that Esther is "well" again and that she has a baby. For a book that is so critical of motherhood and the options afforded to women, Esther's confession is curious. However, it makes sense considering that during Plath's historical moment, becoming a mother was seen as the ultimate success for a woman. This textual blip signals that Esther has survived her ordeal.

This unusual moment is the only time we get a glimpse of present-day Esther. The rest of the novel details how she suffers a nervous breakdown, struggles with her mother, contemplates and eventually attempts suicide, is hospitalized at a psychiatric facility, and attempts to recover and reintegrate into society. It is a mental health coming-of-age story; Esther goes on a journey from suffering a severe depressive episode to eventually working toward recovery and mental health. Along the way, she makes choices that will lead her to the life and identity she wants.

However, the concept of choice and its illusory nature is also something that Esther must contend with. One of the most oft-quoted scenes in the book takes place as Esther tries to figure out how her life should proceed. She imagines herself sitting at the base of a fig tree, with each fig representing a different opportunity: "I saw my life branching out before me like the green fig tree in the story. From the tip of every branch, like a fat purple fig, a wonderful future beckoned and winked." These futures include becoming a professor, an editor, a poet; traveling the world; dating interesting men; and even being a crew champion. But Esther can't pick a fig: "I saw myself sitting in the crotch of this fig tree, starving to death, just because I couldn't make up my mind which of the figs I would choose."

Plath indicates that Esther doesn't actually feel like any of these choices are attainable for her, that choices for women during this period are fantasies: "At best, then, the process of choice for Esther has been circumscribed by societal rules and expectations—rules and expectations that tell her to be one, and only one, thing, despite her own inclinations. At worst, the process of choice is completely denied to her" (Badia, 2006, p. 133). Esther, who wants it all but fears she will fail, has been set up for failure by the limited choices available to women at the time.

Conformity Culture

In the 1950s, conformity culture was strictly promoted. During Plath's internship at *Mademoiselle*, she was expected to wear certain clothing and behave in a certain way: like a lady. Conformity culture was encouraged through dress as well as behavior. But cracks were starting to show. Plath may have looked conventional, but she was intellectually progressive and adventurous, and disdainful of the performances she had to put on (Winder, 2013, p. 170). In this way, *The Bell Jar* is about one woman trying to rebel against conformity culture but finding it too omnipresent.

Esther Greenwood appears to be having the time of her life, but underneath the façade she is dangerously depressed: "I was supposed to be having the time of my life," Esther narrates. But she's not. "Look what can happen in this county, they'd say. A girl lives in some out-of-the-way town for nineteen years, so poor she can't afford a magazine, and then . . . she wins a prize here and a prize there and ends up steering New York like her own private car. Only I wasn't steering anything, not even myself. . . . I felt very still and very empty." By showing that appearances aren't what they seem, Plath criticizes the cultural norms of the time, indicting conformity culture for making young women physically and mentally ill.

One of the main cultural norms Plath criticizes is the sexual double standard of heteronormative dating culture. She does this through her portrayal of Esther's boyfriend Buddy Willard, who is a stereotypical "nice, young man" in medical school with a bright future that ostensibly includes Esther as his virginal bride. But Esther can barely contain her contempt for Buddy—especially once Buddy confesses that he has already been sexually active.

Buddy's confession contributes to Esther's self-destructive path; it fills her with rage that not only is Buddy allowed to engage in sexual activity but that he has made Esther feel foolish: "From the first night, Buddy Willard kissed me and said I must go out with a lot of boys, he made me feel I was much more sexy and experienced than he was. . . . Now I saw he had only been pretending all this time to be so innocent." Buddy's hypocritical attitude and behavior enrages Esther, who explains that she decided to "ditch" him "not because he slept with that waitress, but because he didn't have the honest guts to admit it straight off to everybody and face up to it as part of his character."

Many of Esther and Buddy's interactions take place in hospitals. He takes her on a date to watch a baby being born, which only depresses Esther as she ponders a future in which she must give up her goals to become a mother. Later, Buddy exposes his penis to Esther so she can "see a man" but Esther only feels even more depressed after she describes Buddy's genitals as "turkey neck and turkey gizzards." Buddy's association with the medical field firmly places him in the same category as the doctor who gives Esther botched electroconvulsive therapy—smug men who ignore when women tell them things.

Buddy continually puts down Esther's love of writing and the arts, and touts science as the only notable pursuit in life. In his pursuit of authority in both the professional and personal world, Buddy is completely ignorant about the effect his actions have on others. Perhaps more humorously, he completely misses that Esther hates his guts.

The bell jar itself refers to a physical object that is used to encase and display another object. For Plath, it is a metaphor for being slowly suffocated by conformity culture and going insane. Throughout the novel, Plath refers to the bell jar either firmly placed around Esther's head or looming nearby as a threat: "because wherever I sat—on the deck of a ship or at a street café in Paris or Bangkok—I would be sitting under the same glass bell jar, stewing in my own sour air." Esther has to learn to reconcile that the bell jar will always be in her life, but that with therapy and other tools, she doesn't have to be its captive.

Domestic Oppression

One of the major issues Esther has to grapple with on her journey is the emphasis 1950s' society places on a woman's role as wife and mother. If Esther's editorship in New York City presents her with images of career women who must
give up marriage and family, Esther's return to the Boston suburbs shows her
images of women who eschewed careers to have babies and take care of the
home. What's missing are women who are able to balance both, women who
have satisfying home lives and meaningful jobs. Once in the suburbs, Esther is
faced with two women who symbolize what she fears most about failure: her
own mother and her neighbor Dodo Conway.

Dodo Conway is described as "grotesque" with her pregnant stomach bulg-
ing, the leader of a small parade of children of "various sizes" with dirty knees
and faces. But she also has a "serene, almost religious smile" that suggests
she is inhabiting another world altogether. Dodo Conway went to Barnard,
Esther says, referring to the prestigious all-women's college in New York
City—and then she married an architect who went to Columbia. Dodo fasci-
nates Esther because she so perfectly embodies her anxieties: a wasted education, a suburban existence, and a gaggle of children she cannot escape for
even a moment.

Esther's mother, who teaches shorthand to make ends meet (a job, but one
that Esther demeans), has raised Esther alone after Esther's father died. She
has tried her best to raise her family and also contribute to the household
finances, but Esther finds her stifling and aggravating. She shares a room with
her mother and feels like she has no privacy in the home; even a nosy neighbor
spies on her, reminding us of surveillance culture. As Esther contemplates how
to kill herself, she decides to hang herself with her mother's yellow, silk bath-
robe cord. While this doesn't work, it does represent how domesticity is literally
strangling Esther.

#MeToo and *The Bell Jar*

Along with Cold War cultural ideals like conformity, *The Bell Jar* also considers
what consent and violence against women looks like during a time before rape
was treated as a serious crime (at least when committed by a white man). Sex
crime law at the time made clear that "uncontrolled desires" (Freedman, 1987,
p. 84) were a motivating factor in sexual assault, placing the blame on women
who incited those urges and offering considerable understanding toward

men powerless to stop themselves from raping women. The recent #MeToo revolution of the twenty-first century, with its emphasis on accountability and power dynamics, would have seemed absolutely foreign to Plath and her contemporaries.

Plath writes about sexual assault in *The Bell Jar*, positioning it as the final straw that causes Esther to have a nervous breakdown. Esther goes out for a night on the town with her friend Doreen and her date. They are meeting a friend of his, a man named Marco. It's partly a setup for Esther, but it becomes clear from the beginning that Marco is a misogynist. Esther even calls him a woman-hater after she observes him at the bar: "I could tell Marco was a woman-hater, because in spite of all the models and TV starlets in the room that night he paid attention to nobody but me. Not out of kindness or even curiosity, but because I'd happened to be dealt to him, like a playing card in a pack of identical cards." Marco puts his hands on Esther's arm tightly, leaving marks. Later, Esther offends Marco by asking about his love life, and he throws her to the ground. He then gets on top of Esther. "'It's happening,' I thought. 'It's happening. If I just lie here and do nothing it will happen,'" Esther says to herself.

Esther's initial reaction to Marco's assault—freezing—is a completely normal way for a person to experience a threat to one's body. But it also speaks to larger issues about how men and women were conditioned to think about sex and power during the 1950s. Esther's experiences, suggests Kate Harding, "penalise her specifically by stripping her of any pretensions to masculine independence, reinforcing her femininity while simultaneously defining it was a cause of pain and vulnerability" (Harding, 2019, p. 181). As Plath's experience of independence in New York comes to a close, she is harshly reminded how the world considers women as disposable and deserving of violence.

Marco calls her a "slut" three times and tears her dress with his teeth. Eventually, Esther manages to fight Marco off by kicking him and punching him. She begins to cry. Marco gets up and wipes his bloody nose. Then he takes the blood and marks Esther's face with it. Esther is clearly traumatized by the sexual assault. Later that night, she goes up to the roof of the Barbizon and throws all of her clothing into the night air. She does not wipe the dried blood off her face, leaving the marks of Marco's attempted rape: "I thought I would carry them around with me, like the relic of a dead lover," she tells herself as she makes her way back home to her Boston suburb, a shell of a person.

Esther does not report that Marco tried to rape her. Such an event would most likely not have been taken seriously during the 1950s—feminist theorists

Figure 4.1 Sylvia Plath in her home at 55 Eltisley Avenue, 1956.
Source: Pictorial Press Ltd / Alamy Stock Photo

of the 1970s only began to lay the foundation of what we now know as rape culture. "Being born a woman is my awful tragedy," Plath writes in her *Journals*. "All is spoiled by the fact that I am a girl, a female always in danger of assault and battery" (*Unabridged Journals*, 2000, p. 77). Plath writes Esther similarly, a young woman with ambitions who is seemingly at the mercy of men who violate or disappoint her—like boyfriend Dick Norton with his double standards about sex and Dr. Gordon who does not listen to her and administers botched electroshock therapy.

The Rosenberg Execution

The Bell Jar begins with a passage that neatly connects mental health with Cold War culture and sets the tone for the rest of the narrative: "It was a queer, sultry summer, the summer they electrocuted the Rosenbergs, and I didn't know what I was doing in New York. I'm stupid about executions. The idea of being electrocuted makes me sick, and that's all there was to read about in the papers. . . ." Esther views the Rosenbergs' execution by electric chair as despicable, which gives you an inkling that she's either not buying into Cold War propaganda or she has an ethical objection to capital punishment.

For Esther, the Rosenbergs' execution represent the height of Cold War paranoia and oppression and her own particular feelings of disorientation.

To this extent, Jo Gill claims, "Plath has more to suggest about this historical event than her character does . . . in Esther's response to the Rosenbergs' trial, Plath depicts her generation's inability to grasp the connection between public events and private life" (Nelson, 2002, p. 25). Additionally, the Rosenbergs' electrocution is an example of foreshadowing—later in the book, Esther undergoes a botched electroconvulsive therapy that leaves her traumatized.

Esther also identifies with the Rosenbergs as people who are seen as others; they have been branded as others because of their Jewishness and Communist ideals in the realm of political theater. She internalizes their struggle and empathizes with their pain: "Esther's emotional identification with the Rosenbergs is based on her sense that she too is capable of looking like the right kind of person on the outside, of appearing to conform to middle-class norms . . . but is in reality the kind of person whose identity is so terrible, so unacceptable to her society, that it would leave her simply no place in it" (Ferreter, 2011, p. 104).

With the Rosenbergs' execution looming over the narrative, Esther introduces us to a world filled with overachieving white women, all struggling to appear perfect. Esther is unkind in her observations, establishing her character as someone who is judgmental and critical of others and herself. Not from money, Esther is also incredibly self-conscious of her socioeconomic status in relation to other, wealthier young women. Esther can't seem to connect with other people and form meaningful friendships and relationships. She is lonely, disillusioned with life, and anxious about the future.

A Mental Health Coming-of-Age Novel

Sylvia Plath might have been trying to write a "potboiler" meant to shock the public, but *The Bell Jar* remains one of the most significant books about mental illness and the mental health system in American literature. Plath's decimation of the mental health system is smart, funny, and still timely enough that the book continues to be reprinted.

During Plath's historical moment, mental healthcare and mental hospitals were radically changing. Consider Ken Kesey's 1962 novel, *One Flew Over the Cuckoo's Nest*, a radically anti-establishment book. While it's unknown if Plath was familiar with Kesey's book (she had already completed *The Bell Jar* in 1961), stories about mental health and hospitalizations had begun to enter popular culture. This was in part due to a burgeoning antipsychiatry movement, which felt that psychiatric treatment was often more damaging than helpful.

Plath never discussed the antipsychiatry movement, but *The Bell Jar* levels criticism at the mental health institutions, which would be the movement's target. Plath's novel is "unmistakably indebted to the popular 1950s mental health narratives and memoirs she called 'potboilers' and to the more highbrow anti-psychiatry protest literature that had begun to be disseminated widely by the time Plath began to draft the novel," Dr. Maria Farland argues. "Plath, like other critics of psychiatry, finds coercive clinical practices . . . disturbing in their brutality and violence. Mental health memoirs sensationalize this violence, whereas other anti-psychiatry protest literature deplores it. Plath's novel straddles these two rhetorical modes" (Farland, 2002). Plath is obviously ambivalent, as at the end of *The Bell Jar*, Plath implies that therapy has helped heal Esther.

A significant portion of *The Bell Jar* takes place in a mental hospital as Esther attempts to recover from her suicide attempt. After Esther is discovered in the crawlspace under her house, having overdosed on pills and thrown up, she is taken to the hospital and admitted for long-term care. At this juncture in the novel, Plath writes Esther as having limited insight into her situation as well as paranoid thoughts. As a narrator, Esther begins to become more unreliable as she struggles with the aftermath of a suicide attempt and still-present depression. She is abusive toward the nurses and acts out on purpose. She thinks other patients are mocking her mother.

As soon as Esther leaves the public hospital and moves into a private hospital, we see a shift. In comparing and contrasting the public hospital with the private one, Plath indicts the capitalist system that makes proper healthcare available only to the wealthy. Indeed, it is only because of Esther's benefactor, Mrs. Guinea—who pays for Esther's stay at the private hospital—that Esther is able to get well: "So Mrs. Guinea had flown back to Boston and taken me out of the cramped city hospital ward, and now she was driving me to a private hospital that had grounds and golf courses and gardens, like a country club, where she would pay for me, as if I had a scholarship, until the doctors she knew of there had made me well," Esther narrates. Without Mrs. Guinea's financial assistance, Esther's mother tells her, she didn't know where Esther would end up.

As Esther continues to improve due to her psychotherapy with Dr. Nolan, a progressive woman, she gets more freedoms. One of the most significant is an appointment with a doctor who will fit her with a diaphragm so she can have sex without worrying about getting pregnant: "I climbed up on the examination table, thinking: 'I am climbing to freedom, freedom from fear, freedom from marrying the wrong person, like Buddy Willard, just because of sex," Esther says. "I was my own woman." With birth control, Esther feels empowered and in control of her future. For Esther, who has been haunted by sexual double standards as well as the threat of pregnancy ending her burgeoning professional life, the procurement of the diaphragm is a huge step toward asserting female agency. As a proto-feminist character, Esther illuminates many ways women are contained by the patriarchy as well as by their own reproductive systems—but she also illustrates how they can achieve freedom over their minds and bodies.

At the end of the novel, Esther prepares to fully reenter society: "There ought, I thought, to be a ritual for being born twice—patched, retreaded, and approved for the road," Esther thinks before she enters the room where Dr. Nolan and other psychiatrists will evaluate her. Here, Esther is trying to think of how to frame her experience in a narrative way; to make meaning of it in a linear fashion. This is very much in line with a traditional coming-of-age story. *The Bell Jar* begins with Esther contemplating the execution of the Rosenbergs and ends with her having survived her own suicide attempt and reentering society as a person who is "cured" (today we might say that Esther is in recovery).

Publication History

Plath did not want her book marketed as autobiography. When it was first published in the United Kingdom in 1963, Plath had chosen the pen name Victoria Lucas—perhaps to distance herself from the material. Thus, *The Bell Jar* should be treated as a fictional account of a woman's descent into mental illness. The publication history of *The Bell Jar* is interesting in its own right. When it was published in the United Kingdom under the name Victoria Lucas, the book received mostly average reviews with some standouts: According to the *New Statesman*, it was a "clever first novel."

When the second UK edition came out in in 1966, there was new context: Plath's name was now on the book; *Ariel* had been released to rave reviews, and Plath's suicide was now well known. Reviewers and readers began to see the novel through the lens of all three of those changes. When the book finally reached American shores in 1971, Plath was now famous for both her suicide and her poetry—and most reviewers were unable to view *The Bell Jar* as a stand-alone novel. Feminist movements in America had adopted Plath as a kind of patron saint, and young women were purchasing her book and finding solace and kinship in its pages (Badia, 2006, p. 129). In reviews, these women are often mocked in a misogynistic way, even called a "cult" (Badia, 2006, p. 130). Because of passionate readers of Plath, *The Bell Jar* transcended from being simply a book into a community.

While our culture has shifted since Plath's time, sexism, rape culture, anxiety about life choices, worry about healthcare, fear of political corruption, and fights with our parents still exist. In some ways, *The Bell Jar* is more relevant than ever as the #MeToo movement continues to draw attention to the prevalence of sexual assault and harassment, and mental healthcare is being treated more seriously but still not seriously enough.

SHORT FICTION AND ESSAYS

Plath wrote what was considered at the time "women's magazine stories." This refers to the implied readership as well as publication venue. Critic Luke Ferreter explains that "there is no one typical kind of women's magazine story during the 1950s. There is a heavy emphasis on love stories, on stories about families and on marriage as the conclusion of the love stories. . . . After love, marriage, and family, religion is the most frequent subject addressed" (Ferreter, 2011, p. 37). In the late 1950s and early 1960s, stories might deal with issues like divorce or unwanted pregnancy—cautionary tales.

Plath was interested in writing for money, and entered and won many contests sponsored by these women's magazines such as *Mademoiselle* and *Seventeen*. For Plath, fiction writing was always bound up with money-making; she saw poetry as art and fiction writing as art that could put cash in her pocket. But Plath's stories didn't always fit in with women's magazine stories' typical formula. Her stories were more complex emotionally and focused on nuance and not-easily-solved conflict. Plath's heroines are often assertive with men and also focused on their own ambitions. However, in order to be published, Plath knew she had to play by the rules that women's magazines established: less assertive women, more stories ending in marriage. So she accordingly wrote some of her fiction to fit in more with them. That doesn't mean, however, that some of Plath's short fiction refuses to delve into complex situations.

"Superman and Paula Brown's New Snowsuit" (1955)

Many of Plath's stories that don't neatly fit into the expectations of women's magazines often deal with overtly political concerns. At Smith College, after her suicide attempt and hospitalization, Plath wrote short stories for a class. One of her stories, "Superman and Paula Brown's New Snowsuit" (1955), focuses on anti-immigrant prejudice and the fear of war. The story, which is told from the first person perspective of a woman looking back on her childhood, is about a child's first experience of cruelty in the form of intimated xenophobia and her disillusionment about justice in the world.

The story is based on an incident in Plath's own life. Plath sets the scene by telling us that the protagonist is looking back on events that happened thirteen years ago in 1939, the year World War II began. The unnamed protagonist has a sense of wonder and awe about the world and dreams of flying and of Superman. But as she is more exposed to the horrors of war abroad and the injustice of neighborhood conflicts, she loses her innocence.

Plath's protagonist is characterized as an outsider and someone who finds solace in fantasy. She plays Superman-type games with one other boy, and their games "made us outlaws, yet gave us a sense of windy superiority" (p. 282). As the war becomes more omnipresent in their lives, their Superman games cease. The protagonist narrates how "the threat of war was seeping in everywhere." A boy at school pretends to be a Nazi. The protagonist's mother and uncle talk about how "Germans in America are being put in prison for the duration" of the war. The children are taken to a movie where Japanese prisoners of war are shown being executed, and the narrator needs to get up and vomit all the cake and ice cream (the trappings of consumer culture) she has been eating throughout the day. After that, the narrator says, "no crusading blue figure came roaring down in heavenly anger." Superman is dead.

Things take an even darker turn for the narrator one day when playing with friends. Paula Brown, a girl who is characterized by the plethora of presents she received for her birthday, signifying her wealth, accuses the narrator of pushing her down in an oil slick in her new snowsuit, ruining it. The narrator was nowhere near Paula when the incident happened, but the crowd of children gathers together to point at the narrator and accuses her of the act. As the narrator runs home, the children throw snowballs at her. She has been scapegoated.

When the narrator arrives home, her mother and uncle unconvincingly say they believe her: "Okay, but we'll pay for another snowsuit anyway just to make everybody happy, and ten years from now no one will ever know the difference." But a new snowsuit will not make things better for the narrator, who goes to bed in despair. "Nothing held, nothing was left. The silver airplanes and the blue capes all dissolved and vanished," she says, and then emphasizes the connection of her experience of being bullied and gaslit with the onset of the war: "This was the year the war began, and the real world, and the difference" (p. 287). With the war, "as well as the injustices committed against German Americans, shatter the narrators sense, which she identifies as a child's sense, of justice" (Ferreter, 2011, p. 113).

"Johnny Panic and the Bible of Dreams" (1958)

Toward the end of the 1950s, another genre of literature became available to women aside from magazine fiction: mental illness stories or "madness narratives" (Hubert qtd. in Ferreter, 2011, p. 43). The more sensational, the better. And they had to have a happy ending in which the protagonist is cured of whatever ails her and reintegrates into society. The classic example of a "madness narrative" that Plath would have read was Mary Jane Ward's *The Snake Pit* (1946). In that novel, the protagonist is institutionalized in a psychiatric facility by her husband and undergoes hydrotherapy, electroconvulsive therapy, psychotherapy, and psychopharmacology. She eventually recovers and leaves the hospital.

In 1948, *The Snake Pit* was made into a successful major motion picture starring Olivia de Havilland. As long as order was restored, mental illness stories seemed lucrative for the entertainment industry. Plath wanted to be a part of that success story, turning her life experience into what would become a madness narrative: *The Bell Jar*. But before *The Bell Jar*, though, Plath wrote another madness narrative, the short story "Johnny Panic and the Bible of Dreams" (1958).

"Johnny Panic" starts off by establishing the narrator as an employee in a generic psychiatric institute. "Every day from nine to five I sit at my desk facing the door of the office and type up other people's dreams," she explains, situating herself as an office drone with a very unusual focus. She's a record-typer, but on her own time she has taken it on herself to also work for a character she calls Johnny Panic. Loosely, Johnny Panic is a kind of god or devil who is responsible for peoples' bad dreams and bad mental health. The narrator's belief that she is the "secretary to none other than Johnny Panic himself" (p. 156) immediately causes us to regard the protagonist as unstable or an unreliable narrator because Johnny Panic does not exist in reality.

"Johnny Panic" is a story about a woman losing reality partially as a result of her mind-numbing clerical work. It's an indictment on the mental health industry as well as the conformity and consumer culture of the 1950s. The protagonist is a "dream connoisseur," establishing her identity as a consumer. She believes she can identify the people who come in for psychiatric help by their dreams; she has feelings of power and grandiosity as Johnny Panic's helper, like she has knowledge of deep, universal truths about the human condition. But her delusions feel more real to her than the bland reality in which she exists. She watches patients who are "cured" leave the psychiatric institute with horror: "The pure Panic-light had left his face. He went out of the office doomed to the crass fate these doctors call health and happiness" (p. 166). Losing the connection with Johnny Panic indicates wellness but also an existence devoid of truth.

When the protagonist is caught sleeping in the office so she can keep writing down patients' dreams all night long, she tells the Clinic Director, "You can't fire me . . . I quit" (p. 169)—the classic line of every frustrated worker in a depersonalized office environment. What happens next is straight out of a nightmare concocted by Johnny Panic: The protagonist is dragged into a room and hoisted on a table, where she is given electroconvulsive therapy.

"Johnny Panic" is a madness narrative that is critical of psychiatry. Tracy Brain explains, "Part of the narrator's 'illness' (or crime) is her disregard for consumer capitalism, her refusal to keep her place in that system. Her interest in patient dreams, as well as her criticism of technology and the havoc it wreaks, is a usurpation of her position in the material economy . . . her wish to 'counteract those doctors' is a transgression of the highest order" (Brain, 2001, p. 97). The narrator is punished with electroconvulsive therapy for this transgression, which foreshadows when Esther Greenwood in *The Bell Jar* is also punished via electroconvulsive therapy for her transgressions (depression, wanting to be a writer, rejecting conformity culture, embracing her sexuality).

"Ocean 1212-W" (1962)

Plath's ode to the sea as well as childhood innocence can be read as a mournful mediation on loss. The essay sets up Plath as born to the sea, so to speak: "Breath, that is the first thing. Something is breathing. My own breath? The breath of my mother? No, something else, something larger, farther, more serious, more weary" (p. 22). As with Plath's poetry, the sea here is characterized as something that can give birth; it has a "motherly pulse." The sea also is ever changing, mutating, and offering up different versions of itself—much like Plath conceived of herself: "Like a deep woman, it hid a good deal; it had many faces, many delicate, terrible veils." Plath identifies with the ocean and understands its power and pull. The sea is benevolent but can also kill.

"Ocean 1212-W" is an example of creative nonfiction. In this memoirist essay, Plath seeks to use material from her childhood to establish a kind of origin story for her genesis as a writer. The piece was commissioned by the BBC as part of a program called "Writers on Themselves," in which writers talk about their influences and experiences. Professor Gail Crowther and archivist Peter K. Steinberg explain, "To realize fully why the piece was written, one must understand that this was a professional, commissioned assignment, written specifically for the national broadcast on the BBC. This was not something spontaneously created, like a poem. . . . Plath thought about the idea for upwards of two months" (2017, p. 24).

At the time she conceived of and wrote the piece, Plath was an American expatriate in England, thinking back on her childhood in New England growing up by the seashore. The title of the piece, which was chosen by the BBC, refers to her grandmother's phone number at her seaside home. The original title was "Landscape of Childhood."

"Point Shirley" is the essay's poetic counterpart, although "Point Shirley" was written earlier, in 1959. "Ocean 1212-W" delves into Plath's childhood experience of growing up alone with the sea as a companion and then experiencing the birth of her younger brother as an invasion: "I hated babies. I who for two and a half years had been the center of my tender universe felt the axis wrench and a polar chill immobilize my bones." The ocean seems to understand Plath's distress and it gives her a gift: a wooden baboon. For the young Plath, it's a totem. The sea "perceiving my need, had conferred a blessing."

Plath writes that as a baby, she crawled straight toward the ocean without any sense of fear. The ocean continues to nurture Plath, even allowing her to almost magically learn to swim. It's a protector, a mother. And then one day she experiences its rage: "My final memory of the sea is violence," Plath writes. Her family boards up windows in preparation of a hurricane and hunkers down in their house until the storm passes the next day: "My grandmother's house had lasted, valiant—though the waves broke right over the road and into the bay." A dead shark is in the geranium bed. Everything is chaos, but her grandmother comes out with her broom to restore order, and "it would soon be right."

The essay ends abruptly because that is how the sea is taken away from Plath with the death of her father: "My father died, we moved inland. Whereon those nine first years of my life sealed themselves off like a ship in a bottle— beautiful, inaccessible, obsolete, a fine, white flying myth." It's odd that Plath does not mention her father at all until this point of the essay; he's an absent presence. She writes of her uncle, her mother, her grandmother, her brother, even her uncle's fiancé. No mention of her father. Perhaps his absence speaks more than his presence. In this essay that clearly genders the sea as female and maternal, the father haunts the story, but Plath refuses him a leading role.

"Snow Blitz" (1963)

An essay about cultural misunderstandings as well as loneliness, "Snow Blitz" was written in January of 1963 during an unusually brutal winter in London. As letters and eyewitness accounts show, Plath, who was living in a flat with her children, Frieda and Nicholas, at the time, was struggling to keep herself optimistic in the face of a looming divorce and creeping depression. Her status as an outsider, separated from her famous British poet husband who was knowingly having affairs, made Plath feel alone and humiliated. Toward the end of her life, Plath was isolated in a foreign country with only a handful of friends, which negatively affected her sense of self and colored her poetry and fiction.

"Snow Blitz" is a darkly humorous essay that conveys Plath's sense of isolation as well as desperate need to belong to a community as an American living in London. The "blitz" in the title refers to the German bombing campaign against the United Kingdom during World War II. The Luftwaffe dropped bombs for about two years, trying to break Allied spirits. However, they failed—and "blitz spirit" is still referenced in the United Kingdom in the context of these attacks as British indomitable will. The blitz had the opposite effect on the British; instead of scaring them, it mobilized and emboldened them. It's probable that Plath was trying to channel this spirit and position herself as another strong Londoner surviving in the midst of an environmental pummeling.

At first, the snow is welcome, a curiosity: "I stumbled out with my bundles. I smiled. Everybody smiled. The snow was a huge joke, and our predicament that of Alpine climbers marooned in a cartoon." But then the snow keeps coming—and things start breaking. Plath finds her bathroom to be a disaster, with dirty water strangely filling up the bathtub. She pleads for help to her house agent (a landlord) but is not taken seriously. Her frustration becomes palpable as water continues to drip, her children break apart their crib, and workers abandon her. The house agent provides her finally with some overly complicated, unhelpful advice.

Plath's descriptions of everyday life as a single mother during a weather crisis are extraordinary. She is handling everything on her own, and you get the sense that she is totally reliant on the kindness of strangers. When there is a power cut, her neighbor isn't able to give her emotional support, but he gives her a hot-water bottle for her children to keep warm: "I wrapped my daughter in a blanket with the hot-water bottle and set her over a bowl of warm milk and her favorite puzzle. The baby I dressed in a snowsuit." The scene shows just how resourceful Plath has to be in order to keep her family warm and content while she grapples with that pressure with only peripheral assistance.

Plath concludes the essay on what she thinks her children will learn from this "snow blitz": "My children will grow up resolute, independent and tough, fighting through queues for candles for me in my aguey old age." Plath might have struggled during the harsh winter onslaught, but she hopes her children, as future Londoners, will gain fortitude.

"Snow Blitz" is a "slice of life" piece or a vignette—a snapshot of a moment. On the surface, the essay is about the foibles affecting a young mother during a winter storm that no one is prepared for. Everything goes wrong before things start to go right. And there is a lesson at the end, a hope that hardship will lead to strength. However, beneath the surface is a darker story about a single mother having a difficult time holding down the fort. Though she gets help, she needs to demand it over and over again. She is confused about British plumbing, and it seems like workers take advantage of her. "But where I come from there is snow every winter and the roofs never leak," she tells the agent's assistant, making reference to the relative comforts of the United States. Her neighbor is helpful but they pass each other in the hall like "sad ships." Alone and raising two small children, Plath is dependent on others for fixing basic necessities such as heating and water.

Plath's short fiction and essays tend to get less attention than her poetry and novel, but they are vital to understanding how Plath's thematic concerns translate into every medium. They can also show us, like her journals and letters, how certain life experiences are written about in nonfiction form and then transformed into fiction as well as creative nonfiction. They can also show us how the conventions of fiction and creative nonfiction allow Plath to access different voices and use different techniques, such as developing dialogue and crafting more detailed settings.

Plath's short fiction and essays also allow us to gain insight into how Plath used comedy in her writing. While we might not initially think of Plath as a comedic writer, her fiction and essays show a wry, dry, and sarcastic comedic voice that we don't necessarily see in a lot of her poetry.

Literary Terms Defined

Antagonist: The character pitted against the protagonist . . . the antagonist is not necessarily a villain.

Characterization: The term *characterization* refers to the various means by which an author describes and develops the characters in a literary work.

Climax: The point of greatest tension or emotional intensity in a plot.

Conflict: A confrontation or struggle between opposing characters or forces in the plot of a narrative work, from which the action emanates and around which it revolves.

Diction: Narrowly defined, a speaker's (or author's) word choice.

Plot: The arrangement and interrelation of events in a narrative work, chosen and designed to engage the reader's attention and interest (or even to arouse suspense or anxiety) while also providing a framework for the exposition of the author's message, or theme, and for other elements such as characterization, symbol, and conflict.

Point of View: The vantage point from which a narrative is told. A narrative is typically told from a first-person or third-person point of view; the second-person point of view is extremely rare.

Protagonist: The most important or leading character in a work; usually identical to the hero or heroine, but not always.

Sarcasm: Intentional derision, generally directed at another person and intended to hurt.

Setting: That combination of place, historical time, and social milieu that provides the general background for the characters and plot of a literary work.

Chapter 5
Plath's Journals and Letters

Sylvia Plath is known just as much for her journals and letters as for her poetry and fiction. Because she saw no real divide between her life and her art, her journals in particular are written with care, as if someone might read them one day. One can easily visualize Plath writing in her journals, dreaming of being a famous poet. They are expressive, highly descriptive, and beautifully crafted. They are also an incredible source of insight into Plath's work. Many scholars use Plath's journals as a way to investigate what was happening in Plath's life when she was working on certain poems—not to read them in a purely biographical manner, but to see what was inspiring, catalyzing, and affecting her as a writer and individual.

Plath's letters work similarly. As a research tool, we can see how Plath negotiated with literary journals such as *The New Yorker* and conceived of her poetry for public audiences. We can also see how stunningly Plath is able to shift her voice for a particular audience. As most Plath scholars have noted, Plath's letters to her mother Aurelia are mostly very cheerful and reassuring, filled with positive news and anecdotes about her children, her poetry, her marriage, and details of her life (what she's eating, how the garden is growing, how her health is). She signs letters to her mother "Sivvy"—an affectionate nickname. It's striking to compare these letters with corresponding journal entries, as they seem written by a totally different person.

AUDIENCE AND SELF-FASHIONING

Plath reported her life differently to her mother than to her private journals and other recipients of her letters, in particular, her therapist. This is relatable to many of us. We all write and present ourselves for different audiences in our daily lives—our teachers, parents, friends, and employers. The diction we use changes based on whom we are communicating with. Sylvia's letters are no different. Plath's journals and letters provide "evidence of Plath's concerns with larger political, historical, and environmental matters—about nuclear fallout, McCarthyism, and social inequality" (Brain, 2006, p. 139). They give us insight into her attitudes toward the people with which she was writing letters, which can help us understand how she navigated issues such as gender and class during her life.

Journaling is often associated with women and inhabits the private world. In Western literary history, there is a long tradition of edging out marginalized voices from more "literary" mediums; women and people of color often had to depend on having their writing "relegated" to diaries and letters and then disregarded. For the most part, white men got books and poetry published. Even during Plath's time, women and people of color experienced more scrutiny when they tried to publish. Journals and letters give us important access to the literary genius within marginalized communities.

Like social media, there is an art to journal writing and epistolary correspondence. There's text and subtext—the concrete symbols, characters, and sentences, and what we read between the lines. People know screenshots are forever. Letters, like DMs, are only as private as the recipient is willing to keep them, and anyone who wrote a letter was aware of such and wrote with this in mind. There's a reason collected letters of famous people sell: they're seen as juicy snippets into the mind—but in reality they can be as staged as fiction.

In Plath's case, because she drew on inspiration from her life, people tend to forget that letters and journal entries can be treated as art objects of their own; "there is a danger . . . of erecting false and overly rigid boundaries between Plath's different types of writings, of believing that the poems could not possibly share qualities with, or even arise from, her epistolary practices" (Brain, 2006, p. 142). So while the journals and letters give us an opportunity to track Plath's progress in her poetry and fiction, they also act as art in their own right. Sometimes, direct sentences are even lifted from Plath's letters and journals and used word for word in her poetry and fiction.

Writing of Plath's self-conception of her journaling practice, Sally Bayley says that "her journal . . . will creatively disrupt and override the negative effects of an oppressive cultural conformity. This, in essence, is Plath's journal creed: a belief system as ambitious as the one she holds for life" (Bayley, 2007, p. 247). Using her journal for a place to express her frustration with the sexual double standards of her time, the conservative political atmosphere that frightened her, and a literary world steeped in misogyny, Plath was articulating the ethos that would inform her poetry and fiction.

Like her journals, Plath's letters give us similar insight into her creative choices—but they also provide a look at her professional choices. In particular, they allow us to see how Plath communicated with others in her field as well as editors at magazines like *The New Yorker*. Plath was a consummate professional: organized, polite, solicitous, and informed. She wanted to be successful and understood how the politics of correspondence would aid her in making contacts and fostering relationships in the literary world. She inquires about job opportunities and applies for fellowships and writing residencies. Plath was not playing around. All of these letters are helpful in approaching Plath's writing practice, as submissions and correspondence are a vital part of establishing a literary career.

WITNESSING THE CREATIVE PROCESS

Students can use Plath's journals and letters in two significant ways: as primary, biographical sources and as vital steps in her artistic practice. Looking at how Plath transforms material from her journals and letters into her fiction and poems gives us valuable insight into her creative process. For instance, we can use Plath's personal writings about the Rosenbergs' execution as primary sources that reveal the historical and political context of her work. Plath's political views about this historical incident as well as how she writes about it in *The Bell Jar* have already been discussed. In Plath's journals, she mentions the Rosenbergs' execution in a June 19, 1953, entry:

> All right, so the headlines blare the two of them are going to be killed at eleven o'clock tonight. So I am sick at the stomach. I remember the journalists report, sickeningly factual, of the electrocution of a condemned man, of the unconcealed fascination on the faces of the onlookers, of the details, the shocking physical facts about the death, the scream, the smoke, the bare

honest unemotional reporting that gripped the guts because of the things it didn't say. (*Unabridged Journals*, 2000, p. 541)

Plath also writes about a woman who told her "with beautiful bored nastiness" she was glad the Rosenbergs were going to die. She writes of the telephones ringing at the office, like it's business as usual, and that nobody is really thinking of the enormity of the situation and the value of human life. "They were going to kill people with atomic secrets," she adds, "So that we can have the priority of killing people with those atomic secrets which are so very jealously and specially and inhumanly ours." Plath is shocked there is "no yelling, no horror, no great rebellion" occurring in protest of the executions.

In 1953, writing in the moment, Plath had not yet experienced the botched electroshock therapy that would connect Esther to the Rosenbergs. In 1961, as Plath was writing the *The Bell Jar,* she had eight years distance from both the execution as well as her nervous breakdown. Critic Robin Peel notes that "Esther speaks unstoppably in Plath's novel, but in a sardonic, cynical and detached voice. It is not the voice Plath used in her 1953 journal" (Peel, 2019, p. 210). By 1961, Peel explains, enough time had passed that people were able to see the McCarthy era as excessive and to make fun of it—albeit, in a dark way (similar to Joseph Heller's 1961 novel *Catch-22*).

By 1961, Plath was able to look back on her personal experiences as well as the historical events that formed her. She uses *The Bell Jar* to turn the Rosenbergs into symbols for nonconformity and martyrs of a corrupt system. The Rosenbergs are punished for their crime of rejecting American culture; Esther, with the botched electroshock therapy, is punished for the same crime (Peel, p. 211). "Then something bent down and took hold of me and shook me like the end of the world. Whee-ee-ee-ee-ee, it shrilled, through an air crackling with blue light, and with each flash a great jolt drubbed me until I thought my bones would break open and the sap fly out of me like a split plant," Esther narrates as she receives the electroshock therapy. "I wondered what terrible thing it was that I had done." Of course, Esther hadn't done anything terrible, but her mental illness makes her believe there is something intrinsically wrong with her and that she does not—and can never—fit in.

WRITING AS AN OUTSIDER

Feelings of being an outsider permeate Plath's journals and letters. Even when participating in an activity as practical as beekeeping, Plath's letters allow us to gain insight into how emotional and psychological anxieties color an experi-ence. Similarly to how Plath wrote about Esther's feelings of alienation from her own life, Plath's poems about bees and beekeeping speak to her alienation in the English countryside. In this section, we see how Plath's experiences of beekeeping, as recorded in her letters, informed her poetic practice.

On June 9, 1962, Plath writes a letter to friends Marvin and Kathy Kane, telling them she and Ted have just become the owners of a beehive given to them by one of the local beekeepers: "We went to the North Tawton bee-keepers demonstration this week. The rector was there, & the midwife. All donned those funny screened hats. . .. Ted & I stood like dummies trying not to get stung. . . . When you see us this fall we may have some home-made honey to offer you. Provided the Queen doesn't scorn our ignorance & Swarm" (*Letters Vol. 2*, 2018, p. 779).

A few days later, Plath wrote to her mother with more detail on the bees (her mother also knew a considerable amount about bees, having assisted her father while he wrote his book on bees). She also tells a story about how the bees reacted to her and Ted, explaining that Ted did not suitably protect him-self with the hat and the bees crawled into his hair and stung him. "I didn't get stung at all," Plath tells her mother rather proudly (*Letters Vol. 2*, 2018, p. 783). By this time, Plath and Hughes's relationship was fraying, and it's tempting to read that Plath's smugness about the bee stings as evidence that the bees liked her better and were plotting against Hughes (as the daughter of a renowned bee expert, why shouldn't Plath have a special relationship with her bees?). In a later letter, we see this thinking continue when Plath's bees turn on her after she knocked over their feeder: "even my beloved bees set upon me today," she tells her mother, adding that she is "all over stings."

Another thing that is striking from Plath's correspondence and journal entries about beekeeping is her lack of confidence about the whole process and how confusing it is. Anyone beginning a new hobby will understand her insecurity. "I feel very ignorant," Plath tells her mother. Plath's feelings of igno-rance come across very strongly in the bee poems she would write later that year—and take on an altogether ominous tone that's missing from her letter and journal writing.

It also becomes clear throughout her letters to her therapist during this time that beekeeping was becoming a lifeline for Plath as she experienced the disintegration of her marriage. She writes about how much she loves bee-keeping and plans to go into business selling honey: "I have kept bees this year, my own hive, & am very proud of my bottled honey, & my stings" (*Letters Vol. 2*, 2018, p. 878).

If what we see from Plath in her journals and letters are her growing confidence about keeping bees and how they become a significant part of how she sees herself as a capable person, how do those feelings and experiences affect her bee poems?

According to Lynda K. Bundtzen, the bee poems can be considered examples of allegory: a story that can be interpreted to reveal a hidden meaning. Set up as a sequence, the bee poems tell a surface story of an apprentice beekeeper learning to manage her hive as well as the beekeeping community. In her lengthy analysis of the bee cycle, Bundtzen offers several possible narrative options: that of a woman who has fallen into the trap of domestic drudgery and is desperate to escape, that of a woman who feels alienated from her adopted home, and that of a writer coming to terms with her powers of creation and destruction (2001).

The bee poems were all written over the week from October 3 to October 9, 1962, while Ted Hughes was packing up his things and getting ready to leave Plath. All the poems are composed in five-line stanzas and are all about the same length. The first poem in the cycle, "The Bee Meeting," begins with the speaker's feelings of vulnerability in the face of the expert beekeepers she is meeting: "In my sleeveless summery dress I have no protection." The beekeepers, all members of the speaker's community, are prepared for the beekeeping meeting in their gloves and veils. The speaker cannot tell them apart, and her anxiety is palpable as she is led around passively to observe the process: "Is it some operation that is taking place?/Is it the surgeon my neighbors are waiting for," the speaker wonders. "Is it the butcher, the grocer, the postman, someone I know?" She can't tell anyone apart—she is the outlier. But the speaker knows that she has to see this through: "I am the magician's girl who does not flinch," the speaker says, comparing the rituals of beekeeping to a performance and her participation as a sacrificial figure. She must learn to manage the bees and her discomfort in order to reap their benefits.

The next poem, "The Arrival of the Bee Box" continues the novice beekeeper's journey. She has acquired a box of bees and now is responsible for their care and productivity. "I have simply ordered a box of maniacs," the speaker says. "They can be sent back./They can die, I need feed them nothing. I am the owner." Here, the speaker transforms the physical act of caring for bees into a meditation on power. The speaker seems to think she has control over the bees, but does she really?

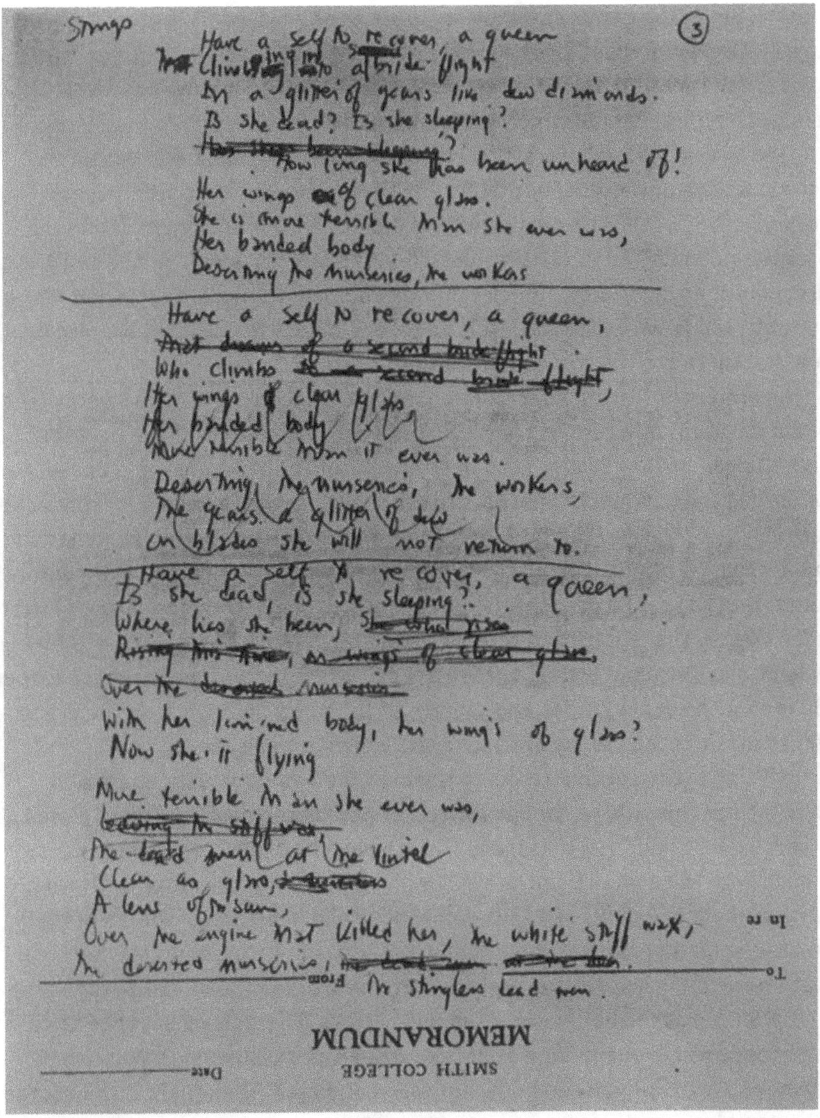

Figure 5.1 Handwritten draft of Sylvia Plath's poem "Stings" on Smith College paper.
Source: University of Illinois

"The Arrival of the Bee Box" with its descriptions of the unpredictable bees might be read as an allegory for writing—that the writer is trafficking in dangerous territory, and she has a choice to repress what is destructive about her writing. But in the poem, she chooses to set the bees free. This reminds us of how Plath characterized the bees in her letters—as friends, as helpers. The bees are the creative spirit that cannot be contained no matter how destructive it might be (Plath's emotionally difficult poetry).

"The Swarm" has an interesting textual history: The poem appears on the contents page of the *Ariel and Other Poems* manuscript with parentheses around it in Sylvia Plath's own hand. She did not include the poem within the manuscript itself. Ted Hughes included it in the U.S. version of *Ariel* when it was first published in 1966 (p. 189). It definitely belongs in the bee cycle, but it's currently unknown why Plath left it out of the poetry manuscript. It's nice to see that there are still some mysteries left to solve.

Regardless of Plath's indecision regarding the inclusion of "The Swarm," the poem functions as a curious transition between "The Arrival of the Bee Box" and "Stings." In "The Swarm," the bees are out of control and a male beekeeper whom the speaker mocks attempts to subdue them with extreme and unnecessary violence. The way the poem begins—"Somebody is shooting at something in our town—" brings to mind the senseless acts of gun violence we are unfortunately used to. And perhaps the poem does attempt to explore acts of historical violence. There are references to Napoleon, "French bootsoles," and Russia, Poland, and Germany. If the bees are a rebellious force and the male beekeeper charged with keeping order, the speaker of the poem sides with the bees and thinks the outsized display of control and violence is ridiculous.

In "Stings," the speaker refers to the hive itself as a domestic space and to herself as "no drudge/though for years I have eaten dust/And dried plates with my dense hair." Here, as many critics have noted, Plath's speaker aligns herself with the aging queen bee in her hive, "her wings torn shawls." Having written about the perils of 1950s domesticity and how it saps women of their creative spirit and renders them solely dull husband-helpers and mothers, Plath transforms her cultural criticism into the story of the queen bee. The last two stanzas can be seen as a feminist victory. The speaker says she has a "self to recover, a queen" and asks, "Is she dead, is she sleeping?/Where has she been,/With her lion-red body, her wings of glass?" Then there is the escape from the hive:

Now she is flying

More terrible than she ever was, red

Scar in the sky, red comet

Over the engine that killed her —

The mausoleum, the wax house.

There are distinct parallels between the queen bee flying out of the hive and the speaker's desire to rediscover herself. The queen bee has left the domestic sphere, and the speaker needs to do the same in order to save herself—no matter how uncertain the future is.

As the closing poem of the cycle, "Wintering" poses a simple question at the end: "Will the hive survive, will the gladiolas/Succeed in banking their fires/ To enter another year?" The speaker seems optimistic that once the patriarchal order has been dissolved, the queen bee and herself will be victorious: "The bees are all women./Maids and the long royal lady./They have got rid of the men."

A writer's journals and letters are more than just an interesting look into their private lives. They are an opportunity to see how works progress over time, how correspondence with different recipients differs. Plath's journal entries and letters about beekeeping can help us understand how her experiences with the beekeeping community, her history with her father, her thoughts about current events, and her unraveling marriage contributed to creating a cycle of poems. Especially with a writer like Plath, who is seen as unusually autobiographical in her poetry and fiction, seeing how she conceives of events from her daily life and then transforms them into art is instructive in how all artists seek to elevate or even exaggerate their own stories into universal stories to which we can all relate.

Chapter 6
Plath's Legacy

Plath is buried in the graveyard at St. Thomas Church in Heptonstall, Yorkshire, England—*Wuthering Heights* country and Hughes's ancestral lands. Hughes chose the location and the epitaph: "In Memory Sylvia Plath Hughes" with her birth and death dates and a quote: "Even amidst fierce flames the golden lotus can be planted." Hughes said the quote was from the Hindu religious text the *Bhagavad Gītā*. It's also possible it came from sixteenth-century Chinese novelist and poet Wu Cheng'en's novel *Journey to the West*.

Like places where other famous writers and artists rest—think of Marilyn Monroe's red-lipstick speckled crypt or Jim Morrison's beer-can littered grave—Plath's grave has a life of its own. A pilgrimage site for writers, people from all over the world come to leave poems, flowers, and pens in memory of Plath. But there's also been troubling vandalism at Plath's grave, showing that some controversies refuse to die and that Plath's legacy spurs people to action.

Beginning in the 1980s, people began to chisel out the "Hughes" from Plath's epitaph. Not just once, but at least three times. People were angry that Plath's grave bore the name of the man who caused her suffering, and insisted that the "Hughes" be removed. No matter how repugnant Ted Hughes's behavior might have been, to desecrate a grave is serious. That it was done repeatedly demonstrates how deeply Plath's work and life story affects people. There was also criticism that Plath had been buried close to Hughes's place of birth in Yorkshire instead of being returned to America, perhaps to be buried near the New England sea she loved so much.

"When I first had the lettering set into the stone . . . the only question in my mind was how to get the name Plath on to it," Ted Hughes said in a 1989 letter written to *The Independent*. "If I had followed custom, the stone would be inscribed Sylvia Hughes, which was her legal name. For her children, it was their mother's name. I was already well aware, in 1963, of what she had achieved under that name, and I wished to honor it."

CULTURAL INFLUENCE

Sylvia Plath remains alive in her work, but she also remains alive in work created by others. Her presence in popular culture as well as literature and art is widespread; she's mentioned in movies like *Heathers* (1989), *Natural Born Killers* (1994), *Ten Things I Hate About You* (1999), and *Spider-man: Homecoming* (2017); in TV shows such as *Jane the Virgin, Law & Order, Pretty Little Liars, Criminal Minds, Gilmore Girls*, and *The Simpsons*; and in songs by musicians such as Lady Gaga and Lana del Rey. In July 2016, there was an announcement that Kirsten Dunst was going to make her directorial debut with a new version of *The Bell Jar* starring Dakota Fanning. However, as of 2020, the project is on hold.

What is it about Plath that resonates in our contemporary moment? One answer is that good literature transcends time and place—it's why we read and re-read *Hamlet* and *Moby Dick* and *Beloved*. Even though all those works occur in different moments and deal with different subjects, there are universal themes that occur in each that we can still relate to: feeling alienated from family, trying to find our purpose, coping with trauma and grief.

But Plath's work keeps getting more and more popular as each generation discovers it. Even from the 1950s and 1960s, her experiences speak to us. And that's in large part because many of the things she wrote about are still problems today. Women are still treated as inferiors to men in many fields and talked down to—Plath would have certainly had a field day with the phrase "mansplaining." Issues relating to childcare and women's ability to work have only been exacerbated due to the COVID-19 pandemic.

With the popularity of the "personal essay industry," however, women's voices have been mocked as they struggle to write about their lives for money on the Internet. Called "navel gazers" or "self-indulgent," writers who carry on the tradition of the Confessional school are often looked down on. For example, writer Elizabeth Wurtzel, who became famous for her nonfiction mental illness narrative *Prozac Nation* (1994), was sneered at for being obsessed with herself—something male nonfiction writers usually never get accused of—even as her book climbed the best-seller charts and helped shatter the stigma of taking antidepressant medication.

These are all reactions to folks breaking boundaries and stigma. After all, sharing one's story and one's experience is a profound way of letting the rest of the world know that you matter and that others matter as well; that they're not alone even if they might feel like it. Confessional writing has always threatened the status quo, and writers continuing the confessional tradition—and updating and making it their own for the digital age—are participating in radical acts of self-affirmation. Today, personal essay, creative nonfiction, and poetry writing are ways for marginalized people to get their stories heard.

THE GROWTH OF PLATH STUDIES

The future of Plath studies is bright. Plath's poetry has been published in over 30 languages (Sampson). There have been at least eight biographies written about Plath, with the most recent (and comprehensive), *Red Comet* by Heather Clark, released in 2020. This most recent biography benefits from archival material that was recently discovered and papers that were released after many years. There still might be even more to discover; that is always the hope—in particular, the "lost" journal from the weeks leading up to Plath's death. As a result of this archival accessibility, Plath studies have expanded to include scholarship on nontextual media such as Plath's paintings, sketches, paper dolls, mixed media collages, and photographs taken of and by her. The archive emphasizes Plath's dual identity as both poet and artist, reminds us of Plath's lifelong devotion to the visual arts, and reinforces critical conceptions of Plath as a writer interested in the material aspects of culture. The archive also introduces us to the Sylvia Plath who was interested in "frivolous" or "low" aspects of culture such as beauty, fashion trends, mainstream cinema, and celebrity gossip—and enhances our understanding of the roles such popular cultural artifacts play in her work.

Plath has always meant a lot to young people—I discovered her work when I was twelve and reading magazine interviews with rock stars I liked. It might have been Courtney Love who mentioned Plath's name, but I immediately thought, "if Courtney Love likes this writer, she must be incredible." And she was. My friends passed around the early published version of her letters. We wrote Plath-esque poetry that was not very good. We were earnest in our affection for this writer who seemed to speak to us as we were being told to take on the world, but also, that thighs were ugly and our sadness was a phase.

FAMILY LEGACY

Plath's story doesn't end with her death. Plath is survived by her daughter, Frieda Hughes, who is a painter and children's book author with British and Australian dual citizenship. Plath's son, Nicholas, was a fisheries biologist who was known for his contributions to stream ecology. He lived in Alaska and taught at the University of Alaska, Fairbanks until 2006. In 2009, he died by suicide, having struggled with depression. Neither Nicholas nor Frieda had children.

Frieda has been a vocal critic of how her mother's poetry has been handled and how people seem to think they have a "right" to her mother. A poem Frieda wrote and published in British magazine *Tatler* harshly condemns a certain kind of reader. The poem is called "My Mother" and it borrows imagery from Plath's poem "Lady Lazarus" in order to show how she feels her mother has been sensationalized and desecrated: "they think/I should give them my mother's words/To fill the mouth of their monster,/Their Sylvia Suicide Doll," Hughes writes. "Who will walk and talk/And die at will,/And die, and die/And forever be dying."

Ted Hughes died of a heart attack in 1998. *Birthday Letters,* his poetry collection dealing with his and Plath's relationship and her death, was published only months prior to his death. The woman Hughes was having the affair with when Sylvia died, Assia Wevill, eventually gave birth to their child, Shura. Both Wevill and Shura died after Wevill gave Shura pills and turned on the gas; she feared Hughes would not commit to her. Having been vilified as the "other woman" for years, scholarship has recently come out celebrating Wevill as a translator and writer in her own right and challenging the patriarchal conditions that led Wevill to believe that she had no future without Hughes as her husband (Goodspeed-Chadwick, 2019, p. 137).

SUMMARY

Plath posthumously won the Pulitzer Prize for Poetry in 1982 for *The Collected Poems.* As the years continue, more of her work is discovered in archives or unexpected places. There are children's books that are now published, such as "The-It-Doesn't Matter Suit." And in 2019, an unpublished short story from

1952, "Mary Ventura and the Ninth Kingdom" was discovered and published. With ever-growing interest in Plath's work, there comes new interpretations; Plath's work has been read with a focus on gender, power, cultural identity, economics, the environment, politics, and other topics.

Plath's work might not speak to everyone. When I was teaching *The Bell Jar* while working on my PhD, I had students who loved it and students who couldn't stand Esther's "whininess." Plath is also not focused on issues that we are more invested in today, such as Black Lives Matter and violence against the LGBTQ community. In her journals, Plath wrote about the evils of apartheid in South Africa and considered herself a liberal-minded person—but she also used racist language in her work that is not possible to defend.

Like with many writers we study in our literature classes, we must grapple with the history of such language as well as the culture that made using racist language seem acceptable. At the same time Plath was writing radical work about women's experiences and mental illness, she had on racial blinders. As a white author, Plath sometimes used the specific experience of nonwhite communities to describe her own emotional pain. In *The Bell Jar,* Esther interacts with Black hospital staff in a way that robs them of their humanity. As Esther recovers from her suicide attempt in the public hospital, she accuses a Black attendant of trying to trick her and purposely kicks him in the leg. Esther is delirious and mentally unwell, but her actions are cruel and purposely aimed at a person of color.

Gail Crowther aptly addresses the racist language in Plath's work in a way that leads us to think about our own blinders: "If Plath, who regarded herself as liberal, who would have been appalled to think she was being racist, used racist language and tropes, then those of us who also inhabit that comfortable space of whiteness need to think about where we are situated in it and what we do about it" (Crowther, 2020). Plath's use of racist tropes and language in her work forces us to examine our own attitudes about race and how race was written about in fiction and poetry of the 1950s and 1960s. This is something that Plath scholarship is only beginning to tackle.

As Plath studies continue to grow, critics and readers look back on previous scholarship and assess what needs to be questioned, further investigated, or tossed out altogether. Scholarship, like fashion, goes through trends. It is not static. And while there are foundational texts, there are also different approaches that critics take when analyzing Plath's work. With this book, I present a more generalized overview of what I think are significant cultural, historical, and biographical contexts. There are books out there that are more focused, and I encourage you to read those if you are interested in getting to know Plath's work better.

SUGGESTED READING

Pain, Parties, Work: Sylvia Plath in New York, Summer 1957, by Elizabeth Winder

These Ghostly Archives: The Unearthing of Sylvia Plath, by Gail Crowther and Peter K. Steinberg

The Other Sylvia Plath, by Tracy Brain

Red Comet, by Heather Clark

The Cambridge Companion to Sylvia Plath, Edited by Jo Gill

Her Husband, by Diane Middlebrook

The headline for the 1981 *The New York Times* review of Plath's *The Collected Poems* reads: "YOU COULD SAY SHE HAD A CALLING FOR DEATH." Let's not do that anymore. Plath wasn't "possessed by a demon." She was an artist. She had a calling for art. She suffered from mental illness during a time in which mental illness was stigmatized and not terribly understood. And as a woman, she suffered from patriarchal violence every step of the way toward achieving her personal and professional goals. Let's center Plath's achievements as we move forward toward a better and more holistic understanding of her influence.

Bibliography

Alexander, Paul. *Rough Magic: A Biography of Sylvia Plath*. New York: Da Capo Press, 1999.

Alexander, Paul, ed. *Ariel Ascending*. New York: Harper & Row, 1985.

Alvarez, A. *The Savage God*. New York: Random House, 1970.

Axelrod, Steven Gould. *Sylvia Plath: The Wound and the Cure of Words*. Baltimore & London: The Johns Hopkins University Press, 1990.

Axelrod, Steven Gould. "The Poetry of Sylvia Plath." *The Cambridge Companion to Sylvia Plath*, edited by Jo Gill, Cambridge: Cambridge University Press, 2006, pp. 73–89.

Badia, Janet. *Sylvia Plath and the Mythology of Women Readers*. University of Massachusetts Press, 2006.

———. "*The Bell Jar* and Other Prose." *The Cambridge Companion to Sylvia Plath*, edited by Jo Gill, Cambridge: Cambridge University Press, 2006, pp. 124–138.

Bayley, Sally. "Sylvia Plath and the Costume of Femininity." Connors, Kathleen and Sally Bayley, eds. *Eye Rhymes: Sylvia Plath's Art of the Visual*. Oxford: Oxford University Press, 2007, pp. 183–205.

"Beautiful Smith Girl Missing at Wellesley." *The Boston Daily Globe*. 25 August 1953: 1+.

Brain, Tracy. *The Other Sylvia Plath*. Essex, England: Pearson Education Limited, 2001.

Brain, Tracy, ed. *Sylvia Plath in Context*. Cambridge: Cambridge University Press, 2019.

Britzolakis, Christina. "*Ariel* and other Poems." *The Cambridge Companion to Sylvia Plath*, edited by Jo Gill, Cambridge: Cambridge University Press, 2006, pp. 107–123.

Browne, Janet. "Darwin and the Face of Madness." *The Anatomy of Madness*. Eds. W.F. Bynum, Roy Porter, and Michael Shepherd. London and New York: Tavistock Publications, 1985.

Bundtzen, Lynda K. *The Other Ariel*. Boston: University of Massachusetts Press, 2001.

Bundtzen, Lynda K. "Plath and Psychoanalysis: Uncertain Truths." *The Cambridge Companion to Sylvia Plath,* edited by Jo Gill, Cambridge University Press, 2006, pp. 36–51.

Churchwell, Sarah. "Secrets and Lies: Plath, Privacy, Publication, and Ted Hughes's *Birthday Letters.*" *Contemporary Literature*, Vol. 42, No. 1 (Spring 2001), pp. 102–148.

Clark, Heather. *The Grief of Influence: Sylvia Plath and Ted Hughes*. Oxford: Oxford University Press, 2011.

———. Red Comet: *The Short Life and Blazing Art of Sylvia Plath*. New York: Alfred A. Knopf, 2020.

Crowther, Gail. "'Fifteen Years between Me and the Bay.': Haunting Places and the Poems of Sylvia Plath." *Critical Insights: Sylvia Plath*. Edited by William K. Buckley. Ipswich, Massachusetts: Salem Press, 2013. pp. 224–242.

Crowther, Gail. "The Comforts of Whiteness." *Gail Crowther*, 31 May 2020, gailcrowther.com/2020/05/31/the-comforts-of-whiteness.

Crowther, Gail, and Peter K. Steinberg. *These Ghostly Archives: The Unearthing of Sylvia Plath*. Fronthill Media, United Kingdom, 2017.

D'Emilio, John, and Estelle B. Freedman. *Intimate Matters: A History of Sexuality in America*. New York: Harper & Row, 1988.

"Day-Long Search Fails to Find Smith Student." *The Boston Morning Globe*. 25 August 1953: 1+.

Ennis, Stephen C., and Karen V. Kukil. *"No Other Appetite": Sylvia Plath, Ted Hughes, and the Blood Jet of Poetry*. New York: The Grolier Club, 2005.

Farland, Maria. "Sylvia Plath's Anti-Psychiatry." *The Minnesota Review*. (2002) pp. 1–13. 12 December 2007. http://www.theminnesotareview.org/journal/ns55/farland.htm

Ferreter, Luke. *Sylvia Plath's Fiction: A Critical Study*. Edinburgh: Edinburgh University Press, 2011.

Field, Douglas, ed. *American Cold War Culture*. Edinburgh: Edinburgh University Press, 2005.

Freedman, Estelle. "'Uncontrolled Desires': The Response to the Sexual Psycho-path, 1920–1960." *The Journal of American History*. Vol. 74, No. 1 (June 1987), pp. 83–106.

Frost, Laura. *Sex Drives: Fantasies of Fascism in Literary Modernism*. Ithaca and London: Cornell University Press, 2002.

———. "Every Woman Adores a Fascist": Feminist Visions of Fascism from *Three Guineas* to *Fear of Flying*. *Women's Studies*, Vol. 29, 2000, pp. 37–69.

Gilbert, Sandra M., and Susan Gubar. *Shakespeare's Sisters*. Bloomington and London: Indiana University Press, 1979.

Gill, Jo, ed. *The Cambridge Companion to Sylvia Plath*. Cambridge: Cambridge University Press, 2005.

Gill, Jo. "*The Colossus* and *Crossing the Water*." *The Cambridge Companion to Sylvia Plath*, edited by Jo Gill, Cambridge University Press, 2006, pp. 90–106.

———. *The Face of Madness: Hugh W. Diamond and the Origin of Psychiatric Photography*. New York: Brunner/Mazel, 1976.

———. *Seeing the Insane*. New York: J. Wiley: Brunner/Mazell Publishers, 1982.

Gilman, Sander L. *Disease and Representation: Images of Illness from Madness to AIDS*. Ithaca: Cornell University Press, 1988.

Graves, Robert. *The White Goddess*. New York: Creative Age Press, 1948.

Grisafi, Patricia. *The Sexualization of Mental Illness in Postwar American Literature*. Dissertation, Fordham University, 2016.

Goodspeed-Chadwick, Julie. *Reclaiming Assia Wevill: Sylvia Plath, Ted Hughes, and the Literary Imagination*. Baton Rouge: Louisiana State University Press, 2019.

Harding, Kate. "'Women-haters Were Like Gods': *The Bell Jar* and Violence Against Women in 1950s America." *Sylvia Plath in Context*, edited by Tracy Brain, Cambridge: Cambridge University Press, 2019. pp. 180–190.

Haslam, Dave. *My Second Home: Sylvia Plath in Paris, 1956*. Manchester, UK: Confingo, 2020.

Hayman, Ronald. *The Death and Life of Sylvia Plath*. Gloucestershire: Sutton Publishing Limited, 2003.

Helle, Anita Plath. *The Unraveling Archive: Essays on Sylvia Plath*. Ann Arbor: University of Michigan Press, 2007.

Holbrook, David. *Sylvia Plath: Poetry and Existence*. London: The Athlone Press, 1976.

Hughes, Ted. *Birthday Letters*. New York: Farrar, Straus and Giroux, 1998.

Kendall, Tim. *Sylvia Plath: A Critical Study*. London: Faber and Faber, 2001.

Koren, Yehuda, and Eilat Negev. *Lover of Unreason. Assia Wevill, Sylvia Plath's Rival and Ted Hughes' Doomed Love*. New York: Avalon, 2006.

Kroll, Judith. *Chapters in a Mythology: The Poetry of Sylvia Plath*. New York: Harper & Row, 1976.

Lant, Kathleen Margaret. "The Big Strip Tease: Female Bodies and Male Power in the Poetry of Sylvia Plath." *Contemporary Literature* Vol. 34, No. 4 (1993), pp. 621–669.

Laplanche, J., and J.B Pontalis. *The Language of Psycho-Analysis.* New York: Norton, 1974.

Locke, Richard. "The Last Word: Beside the Bell Jar." 20 June 1971. *The New York Times* on the Web. 12 September 2007. <http://www.nytimes.com/books/98/03/01/home/plath-last.html>

Malcolm, Janet. *The Silent Woman.* New York: Random House, 1993.

Manners, Marilyn. "The Doxies of Daughterhood: Plath, Cixous, and the Father." *Comparative Literature*, Vol. 48, No. 2 (Spring 1996), pp. 150–171.

Middlebrook, Diane. *Her Husband.* New York: Penguin Books, 2003.

———. "The Poetry of Sylvia Plath and Ted Hughes: Call and Response." *The Cambridge Companion to Sylvia Plath,* edited by Jo Gill, Cambridge: Cambridge University Press, 2006, pp. 156–170.

Murfin, Ross, and Supryia M. Ray. *The Bedford Glossary of Critical and Literary Terms.* Boston: Bedford/St. Martin's, 1998.

Narbeshuber, Lisa. "The Poetics of Torture: The Spectacle of Sylvia Plath's Poetry." *Canadian Review of American Studies* Vol. 34, No. 2 (2004), pp. 185–203.

Nelson, Deborah. *Pursuing Privacy in Cold War America.* New York: Columbia University Press, 2002.

———. "Plath, History, and Politics." *The Cambridge Companion to Sylvia Plath,* edited by Jo Gill, Cambridge: Cambridge University Press, 2006, pp. 21–35.

Newman, Charles, ed. *The Art of Sylvia Plath.* Bloomington: Indiana University Press, 1971.

Park, Jooyoung. "'I Could Kill a Woman or Would a Man': Melancholic Rage in the Poems of Sylvia Plath." *Women's Studies*, Vol. 31, No. 4 (Jul/Aug 2002), pp. 467–497.

Peel, Robin. *Writing Back: Sylvia Plath and Cold War Politics.* Madison, NJ: Fairleigh Dickinson Press, 2002.

———. "'Body, Word, and Photograph': Sylvia Plath's Cold War Collage and the Thalidomide Scandal." *The Journal of American Studies,* Vol. 40 No. 1 (2006), pp. 71–95.

———. "*The Bell Jar,* the Rosenbergs, and the Problem of the Enemy Within." *Sylvia Plath in Context,* edited by Tracy Brain. Cambridge: Cambridge University Press, 2019, pp. 203–212.

Pfister, Joel. "Glamorizing the Psychological: The Politics of the Performances of Modern Psychological Identities." Inventing the Psychological, edited by Joel Pfister and Nancy Schnog. New Haven: Yale University Press, 1997, pp. 167–213.

Pfister, Joel, and Nancy Schnog, eds. *Inventing the Psychological.* New Haven: Yale University Press, 1997.

Plath, Aurelia Schober, ed. *Letters Home.* New York: Harper & Row, 1975.

Plath, Sylvia. *The Collected Poems.* New York: Harper & Row, 1992.

———. *Johnny Panic and the Bible of Dreams.* New York: Harper Perennial, 2000.

———. *The Unabridged Journals.* New York: Anchor Books, 2000.

Presley, Nicola. "Plath and Television." *Sylvia Plath in Context*, edited by Tracy Brain, Cambridge: Cambridge University Press, 2019. pp. 180–190.

Ramazani, Jahan. *Poetry of Mourning: The Modern Elegy from Hardy to Heaney.* Chicago: University of Chicago Press, 1994.

Rose, Jacqueline. *The Haunting of Sylvia Plath.* Cambridge: Harvard University Press, 1992.

Rosenblatt, Jon. *Sylvia Plath: The Poetry of Initiation.* Chapel Hill: The University of North Carolina Press, 1979.

Ries, Lawrence R. *Wolf Masks: Violence in Contemporary Poetry.* Port Washington, WI: Kennikat Press Corp., 1977.

Shorter, Edward. *A History of Psychiatry.* New York: John Wiley & Sons, Inc. 1997.

Shorter, Edward, and David Healy. *Shock Therapy: A History of Electroconvulsive Treatment in Mental Illness.* New Brunswick: Rutgers University Press, 2007.

"Sleeping Pills Missing with Wellesley Girl." *The Boston Herald.* 26 August 1953: 1+.

Smith College. "Information Sheet: Posture Pictures Article in *The New York Times*." 25 January 1995.

"Smith Student Found Alive in Cellar." *The Boston Evening Globe.* 26 August 1953: 1+.

Steinberg, Peter K., and Karen V. Kukil, eds. *The Letters of Sylvia Plath Volume 2: 1956–1963.* New York: Harper Collins, 2018.

Stevenson, Anne. *Bitter Fame.* New York: First Mariner Books, 1998.

Strangeways, Al. "'The Boot in the Face': The Problem of the Holocaust in the Poetry of Sylvia Plath." *Contemporary Literature*, Vol. 37, No. 3 (November 1997), pp. 370–390.

Tuite, Rebecca C. "Plath and Fashion." *Sylvia Plath in Context*, edited by Tracy Brain. Cambridge University Press, 2019, pp. 126–137.

Van Dyne, Susan. *Revising Life*. Chapel Hill: The University of North Carolina Press, 1993.

Wagner-Martin, Linda. *Sylvia Plath: A Life*. New York: Simon & Schuster, 1987.

Wagner-Martin, Linda, ed. *Critical Essays on Sylvia Plath*. Boston: G.K. Hall & Company, 1984.

"Wellesley Girl Found in Cellar." *The Boston Herald*: 27 August 1953: 1+.

Whitfield, Stephen J. *The Culture of the Cold War*. Baltimore: Johns Hopkins University Press, 1991.

Winder, Elizabeth. *Pain, Parties, Work: Sylvia Plath in New York, Summer 1953*. New York: Harper Collins, 2013.

Wilson, Andrew. *Mad Girl's Love Song*. New York: Scribner, 2013.

Yosifon, David, and Peter Stearns. "The Rise and Fall of American Posture." *The American Historical Review*. Vol. 103, No. 4 (1998), pp. 1057–1095. heteron

Index